The Undertaker's Son

Book 1
Silent Harvest Series

by

Elizabeth Fortini

Elizabeth Fortini

Edited by
Cornel Rosario

Cover design by
Eva M. Fortini

And a special thanks to
Professor Daniel Becker

Cover model
Matthew Corrigan at
The Gardens of Stone Bank, WI.

Manufactured in the United States of America.

Acknowledgements

The author would like to thank God for being the main factor in making this novel a reality. She also would like to thank her editor, Cornel Rosario, who has helped her through the process of publishing, and Eva Fortini, freelance photographer and sister, for being so patient in taking the cover photo.

Lastly, she would like to extend her gratitude to her family (especially her Mom and Dad) and friends for being so supportive of her.

For my cousin Yana Fairman, USAF cadet.
I am so proud of you!

Chapter One

*N*ighttime overtook the day as the last glimpse of the sun's rays dipped behind the golden valleys of the peaceful countryside. Overhead, the birds found rest in their wooded dens, while the creatures below lurked about the land until sleep overcame them. Only the nocturnal creatures were left to take dominion over the night, as well as those ladies and gentlemen who found their enjoyment by engaging in late-night festivities.

When all signs of day had completely gone and the dark lingered on into the midnight hour, the wind began to rise up against the trees and the clouds consumed the glorious heavens. The air then eavesdropped on families' conversations, friends' quarrels, and the graceful sounds of Renaissance music coaxing any listeners to indulge in dance.

It was a typical evening in the spirited village, but a high gust of wind suddenly emerged, hindering the approaching sounds of a desperate soul as it galloped through the treacherous wind currents. When the air finally calmed itself, the sound of the horse's hooves ruled the night, refusing to submit to the evening's stillness.

The darkness was so overwhelming in these parts that only someone who truly knew the roads could accomplish a safe arrival. Indeed, the rider was more than familiar with the path, having traversed it since her youth. Oftentimes she had enjoyed pleasant excursions with friends to the Songbird Village which rested just a mile from their hometown, Denny's Grove. Nature's beauty pervaded the entire area that surrounded Rothbury, and those that took refuge in these parts drew pride from that splendor.

As she neared the halfway point to her destination, little peeks of the moon's light emerged from behind the clouds to reveal a little of the traveler's identity. The woman, who rode bareback upon a black stallion, had a sense of anxiety on her face as she scanned her surroundings from left to right, as if searching for a moving target. Her green eyes shimmered in the soft rays that occasionally passed through her pupils, as her dark hair fell behind her ears as if to wave its good-byes to the land it had just left behind. She was plain, to say the least, although she did reveal a hint of inner beauty through her otherwise unassuming exterior.

As she approached the cemetery, she abruptly ordered her horse to a stop. Obediently, the animal gracefully came to a halt, giving the woman a brief respite from the cold air whipping into her face.

As she looked about, she could see that winter was just retreating from the area, gauged by the occasional patches of grimy snow still on the road sides. The weather during the day had become more and more bearable and some of the trees were even showing signs of spring.

She did not delight in this, though, as she removed her glance. She turned her head slightly to her right, staring out towards the headstones that floated within the fog and darkness, and fixed her eyes upon them. She showed no sadness, no apprehension, nor any emotion for that matter, and just kept her gaze. She merely continued to stare, as if speaking to the graveyard with her eyes, and sighed.

Cold death seemed to rise from the ground, consuming every fiber of the woman's body, and hinder any other noise from her ears. The strange feeling, however, did not last long as her trance was lifted by the sound of a fiddle in the distance. A coughing fit then overcame her, now reminding her of why she had come in the first place.

When she had recovered, she readied herself for departure when a wolf emerged from the night mist, blocking her path. "Go away. Shoo!" she called out to it. But it was far from moving. It began to growl and foam at the mouth, displaying its pearly white teeth to rider and stallion. With the sound of the animal's displeasure echoing in their ears, now four more members of the wolfpack emerged, smacking their lips and gnashing their teeth.

The woman leaned forward and gently put a hand to her horse's face. Bending down towards its ear, she whispered, "Wilbur, I suggest we get out of here." She then gave it direction to do so, but the wolves spooked the horse, causing him to rise up and fall back down to the ground. "Whoa there, boy!" the woman cried out as she tried to get her horse under control. A bite to its leg by one of the wolves, however, sent the horse for the hills, throwing off its rider, as it galloped away into the night. Three of the five wolves ran after Wilbur, while two stayed with the startled woman, waiting for her next move. She was too alarmed to do anything other than stare down her predators. Her eyes darted back and forth between their bubbling mouths and bony exteriors. She felt so helpless, knowing that if she screamed they'd surely pounce.

But it appeared that their hunger was too great, for they both made a jump at her. She threw her arm over her face and cried out. She didn't feel any of her flesh torn, nor any scratches or teeth marks from the creatures. Instead, she heard one of them yelp, raising all sorts of questions in her mind. As she looked up, she saw a man warding off the beasts with a shovel. He hit them violently, the first over the head and the second on its rib cage. The beatings caused did not defeat the animals completely. Rather, they ran off yipping in pain, leaving a trail of blood behind them.

When things had settled down, the woman peered awestruck in the direction of the beastly creatures, then at the man who had saved her life. She rolled her eyes up to him, seeing his grip tightly maintained on his shovel, his body firmly turned in the direction of the retreating, whining animals. Within a minute or two, though, their eyes met.

Now able to see his face, she saw that the man was quite young. His hair was a blondish-brown color and his eyes were a fiery brown. His body was well-built, most likely the result of his work in the cemetery.

He didn't speak a single word, which put off the woman a bit. He did not offer a hand to help her up nor avert his eyes. He just stared at her, as if wondering what she was doing on his land.

The woman put aside her fear, however, since she felt safe with this man, and pushed herself up to face him, first brushing herself off before any words were spoken between them. She thought she would have to be the first to say something, but to her surprise, the man abruptly spoke, not in anger, but not in a cheery tone either.

"What are you doing here?" he asked in a solemn and slightly Scottish tone. The woman slowed her heart, since it had been beating violently against her chest because of the wolf scare. She made eye contact with him, seeing how serious he was.

His eyes frightened her a bit, but she closed her own to compose herself, and opened them again to say, "I'm on my way to Denny's Grove. My father just recently passed."

"Ah," said the man, suddenly comprehending, "you're Miss Rosemary Wheaton."

A little shocked that he knew her, she choked on her words and replied, "Y-yes, but most people call me Mary." Mary didn't know if her words angered the man or were of no interest to him, because he just continued to stare at her.

Keeping her ground was a task in itself, since his somber demeanor made her uncomfortable, but she did what she could to think of something to say to him. Perhaps she could ask him to escort her into town. What a trip that would be! But she was dumb for words; thousands passed before her tongue, yet none would come forth.

Finally, courage came to her, and her ability to articulate returned. After minutes of awkward staring, Mary took in a deep breath and said, "Thank you, sir, for saving me." But the man's eyes averted as he looked out into the direction of the town, listening for any howling noises in the distance. "What a strange fellow," Mary thought.

Suddenly, he jerked his head toward her, as if he had heard what she was thinking, and looked intently at her. "I wouldn't have to, if you had not troubled yourself to travel alone," he firmly declared. Mary was taken aback by the sudden sharpness of his voice.

"I admit," she said in the most even tone she could muster, "I slipped out of the house when I was advised not to. You see, I've been ill and confined for so long that I didn't care if I died of a chill. I've already missed my father's funeral and just had to return home." The man's eyes fell to the side, seeming to cast in indifference. This greatly amazed her.

"Please, sir," she pleaded. "May I trouble you for a ride into town?"

Turning his fiery brown eyes towards her green, his glance seemed to lighten. His shovel fell from his shoulders and without saying a word, his look signaled her to follow him. Submissively, she did so, trying not to think of how the journey home would be.

Leading her to the cemetery's gate, he opened it for her and she entered. He then led her through the fog-enveloped grounds to a stable under a large elm tree. There, a hearse rested beside two healthy-looking, black horses. She stared at the vehicle, watching as he passed around her to toss aside his shovel, and he quickly prepared the hearse for the upcoming ride. In a matter of minutes, they were off and Mary was more than grateful.

Normally, she delighted in lively conversation with her drivers, but this was one man she was hesitant to even look at. The entire journey was made in dead silence. The man focused his attention on his driving, maintaining his seriousness through it all. The moment she would see her home could not come soon enough. Traffic was non-existent, save for a few pedestrians, so the trip to Wheaton Manor was a quick one.

When the hearse had halted in front of the woman's home, she jumped off and curtsied to him. His face didn't change for a single instant. He merely glanced at her, returned his attention to his horses, and drove off.

All her experiences of that day had been nothing if not strange as she watched him drive out of the gate. When he had disappeared down the road, Mary turned her gaze towards her home.

Chapter Two

*M*ary's entrance seemed to surprise everyone. They were overjoyed to see her, though Dolly Peyton, the girl's childhood nurse, scolded her for rashness.

"Has senselessness overcome you?" the woman cried as she prepared a hot towel for her. "The Wellingtons kept you locked up for a reason. Why must you travel in such cold weather when you were just getting better?"

Mary smiled. "I missed Father's funeral," she declared with a cough. "I would only suffer further if I had to wait another month for a visit."

"You might be confined longer because of that little stunt," Dolly replied firmly. "Miss Mary, you're only nineteen; you have a full life ahead of you. Take care of yourself, for heaven's sake!"

"Pish-posh," the stubborn girl responded. "I've had a good life. Besides, it's worth dying if it means seeing Father again."

"What makes you think you'll both be in heaven?" Dolly teased. "Your entry there would be such blasphemy against God's good design." The girl grinned.

"Any person that can see through my devilish character as well as you, Dolly, must have already had some experience herself in the arts of which you charge me," Mary giggled.

The nurse shook her head while she applied an ointment-like substance on the girl's skin. Rising to leave, she was almost at the door when Mary called out to her, "I love you, Mrs. Peyton!"

"Stand behind me, Satan!" she replied in a sarcastic tone of voice and left the room, shutting the door behind her.

Indeed, it would be a while before Mary would be allowed to leave her chamber. She was just happy that she was able to be ill at home. She had felt imprisoned at the Wellington's residence in Osiris Creek, though she knew they'd meant well.

Drifting into sleep, Mary's mind revisited her conversation with the servants the previous night. She had just jumped off the hearse and watched it leave through the gates, before she knocked on the manor door.

"Miss Wheaton!" one of the older servants had cried out. "What are you doing here?! We were informed that you were ill!" From her coughing, the servant could see that Mary was still not completely free of her ailment.

Mary stumbled in, holding her handkerchief to her face, and wiped her nose before inquiring, "Where's Dolly?" Those who had gathered there exchanged glances.

"She's sleeping at the moment," a youngster chimed in. "Would you like me to wake her, Miss Mary?"

"No thank you, Benny," Mary replied with a sneeze. Turning to the servant who had opened the door for her, she requested, "Mr. Lou, could you please get me a chair?"

He left immediately, as various others attended to her, and soon returned with a chair from the dining room. Lightly setting it down near the stair's landing, he asked if she needed anything else. "No, no," she replied, as she sat down. "I'm a little parched, but not especially hungry."

"Not very hungry, eh?" he returned. "You rode nearly fifty miles! And how is it that Master Denzel permitted you to leave in your condition?"

"It's as if you think I'm dying," she said with a toss of her head. "It's only a cold, Mr. Lou. It's not like that severe monster I contracted when I was twelve. Besides, who said Mr. Wellington allowed me to leave? He wouldn't even let me adjust my pillow without having one of his servants intervene."

Just then, Benny returned with a glass of water. Sitting up, she gratefully took it. Mr. Lou watched as she downed the entire glass, then, taking the empty glass from her, he questioned, "Are not the Wellingtons in a mad frenzy, trying to find you?" Mary waved her hand at him.

"I'm sure they know where I've gone," she declared nonchalantly. "I knotted my sheets together when no one was looking and threw them out the window. I'm rather surprised no one saw me."

The servant smiled. "Do you wish to write them, Miss?"

"Ah, Wadsworth Lou," Mary beamed, rising from her seat, "you know me all too well."

With that, Wadsworth motioned a servant to take the chair while he escorted Mary to the drawing room. As they entered, the girl saw how the room kept to its original state since her last being there. The furniture, decorations, and color were all unchanged. And, as expected, her father's writing desk was positioned close to the window.

She slowly sat down, immersing herself in her memories, and lightly touched the wood where her father wrote his business letters. He often told Mary how her mother would move the small desk near the window from the far corner of the room just so she could see him returning home. Servants would come in, scratching their heads, wondering how the desk continued to move to the same spot near the window, and would carry it over to the corner, only to see it back by the window the very next day.

The girl yearned for her mother, who had died when she was born. Her father often spoke of her; he was so descriptive in his words about her that it was as if the woman was right there with them. She sounded elegant and beautiful, yet a bit of a handful at times.

"Your mother," Mr. Wheaton would say, "was always the talk of the town. She would run in the mud before church and return home with no time to change. She had to go, just as she was, and her mother and father were horrified to see it! But when it came down to serious matters, your mother was the best. She loved prayer and loved to sing, although her voice was always a bit off-key, and her words always incorporated God and the family. But perhaps it's best that you didn't meet her, since she would put more ideas in that little, mischievous head of yours!"

Memories were spoken of and made in this room as Mary reached for a quill. It was hard to believe that her best friend had died without proper good-byes exchanged. A letter could describe feelings, but it could not express them the way that physically seeing that person does.

But Mr. Wheaton knew that his daughter loved him. He wished for her presence, but he was the ultimate factor that kept the girl away from him in his final hour. "Why would I endanger my only child's health?" he said to Dolly with the little strength he had left. "And for what? To watch her father die? No, instead of death looking upon death, I'd rather have death die apart from life. My Rosemary loves me and that's all the comfort I need for a happy death."

Breathing an unnoticeable sigh, the girl began to write to the Wellingtons concerning what she needed sent to Wheaton Manor. Mr. Lou, watching over her as she wrote, decided to sit on the nearby sofa, struggling to ward off sleep as he waited.

For nearly five minutes, the girl wrote without any distractions. She first apologized to the family for fleeing, explaining her reasons for doing so, and asked them not to worry on her account. But when she came to the part where she needed to request her things, Mr. Lou suddenly came to her attention. He had been falling in and out of sleep. Now awakened by his own loud snoring, he sat up, fatigued.

Having seen enough, Mary smiled and returned to her work, saying, "I do not need a chaperone for writing my letter. Go to sleep, Wadsworth. I'm able to care for myself."

Shaking himself of his weariness, the servant responded, "With all due respect, Miss, I would rather remain here with you."

"Very well," Mary uttered, without putting up an argument. "But do know that since I am the sole heir to my father's estate, the town will soon be seeking me out when they hear about my return."

This news got Wadsworth's attention. He then reconsidered his words. "Perhaps I should get some rest," he decided, rising from his seat. Before exiting, he turned, a hand on the doorknob, and said, "You are most certainly of the master's origin. It is good to have you back, Miss Mary. Goodnight."

"Goodnight, Mr. Lou," the girl smiled. And with that, the servant was out the door.

About twenty minutes after Mr. Lou's departure, the girl finished her letter and retired to her chamber. She refused any meal and slept late into the next day. When she finally awoke, Dolly was standing beside her bed with some news.

"Mistress," Dolly said in a soothing tone. "Someone has called upon you."

"I don't want to see anyone today," the girl answered sleepily, throwing her head back upon her pillow. "Tell them to go away, Dolly."

"I would, if it were a man," the nurse replied sassily, "but Miss Greenwood wishes to see you." Instantly, Mary leapt out of bed, nearly falling to the floor in her haste, and ran about her room looking for clothes. "Calm yourself!" the nurse cried out to her. "You're still ill!"

"Maybe so," Mary said, throwing various garments around, "but I have not seen Morgan since my fourteenth year."

"I thought you did not wish to see anyone today," the nurse taunted. "I should tell her to go."

"You'll do no such thing!" the girl gently reproached. "Do not joke about this!" Dolly snickered.

"It's amazing how quickly one recovers from a nasty sickness when good news comes their way."

This girl, whom Mary was anxious to see, had been her childhood friend as long as she could remember. Morgan was a breath of fresh air amidst all the arrogance that existed within Denny's Grove. Since there was not much for the townsfolk to do, they thrived on gossip. It was no wonder that it didn't take long for someone to hear of Mary's arrival.

Morgan was a pretty girl. She had beautifully luscious, red-golden locks that fell ever so exquisitely about her. Her freckled face was always bright and cheery, while her deep, brown eyes always sparkled. Her older brother, who would often join in on the girls' festivities, was a handsome young man. His hair was a blistering red, and his eyes, too, were a deep brown.

Finally ready to present herself, Mary descended the stairs and happily greeted her friend Morgan who waited with her brother in the parlor. The pair appeared as handsome as ever, their smiles endearing and their laughs captivating. Morgan joyfully grabbed her friend's hands and kissed her on the cheek. "Oh happy day that the rumors in this town are true!" she proclaimed with a cheery smile.

She reluctantly released Mary, so that her brother could offer his welcome. Coming towards him, Mary curtsied, while Timothy bowed to her. "Oh, Mr. Greenwood," Mary said a bit disappointedly. "You are but the same. Am I to receive no acknowledgement from you?" Smiling broadly, Timothy opened his arms and received Mary.

"Leave it to you to spit upon tradition," Timothy teased.

After pleasantries had been exchanged, Mary offered her friends a seat so they could chat about the happenings since her departure to the Wellingtons. After all, Mary had been absent from her home for five years!

"You might think I'm going to express my astonishment in seeing you here," Morgan started, once they were situated, "but I knew that not even the plague could keep you from visiting. How are you anyway, dear?"

"Just a slight fever," Mary replied, ringing the bell for tea, "nothing too serious." She waited while the servants placed the tea tray on the table, before continuing. "If only I would have escaped two days earlier, then I could have at least attended Father's funeral. How was it, Morgan? Was the weather as horrid as he desired?"

"Yes," Morgan responded, taking a sip of her drink. "The weather was horrid unpleasant, but as we exited the kirk and entered the grounds for the burial, the lightning ceased and only the rain remained. It was quite a peculiar thing, wouldn't you say, Timothy?"

"Quite peculiar," Timothy agreed. "But I see how you fret, Miss Mary. You needn't worry yourself. Morgan was with him when he passed."

Casting her glimmering eyes in Morgan's direction, emotion overcame Mary as she set down her tea. "You have no idea how relieved I am to hear this," she said with little tear drops forming in her eyes. "I thank you from the bottom of my heart, my dearest friend. How did he go? Was it peaceful? I most certainly hope it wasn't painful."

"As you've said," Morgan assured. "He was so tranquil with every word that he spoke, that each one would have been a fitting way to conclude one's life. But what he finally said to me I was to repeat so that you may hear it also." Clasping Mary's hand, Morgan closed her eyes, remembering the scene as if she were there that very moment. She echoed Mr. Wheaton's words to a tee as she lifted her head, replaying the scene as if in a dream.

"Morgan," Mr. Wheaton wearily called out, with an outstretched hand. Slowly, the tear-filled girl inched her way over to the dying man's bedside and grasped his hand. She stilled its quiver with her other hand as her eyes met his. "Morgan," Mr. Wheaton said again. "I want you...to tell my daughter...these words exactly."

"What are they?" Morgan choked, tears dropping to her hands. "I promise I will relay them just as you have said."

Mr. Wheaton did not speak for a minute, causing Morgan to think that he had gone before saying what he wished to, but she felt a weak pulse against her hand, which reassured her otherwise. "Tell Rosemary," the father spoke again, "that I love her. She is the most precious gift that God has ever given to me. Life has passed, so that new life could have its chance in this world. Her mother could have easily saved herself if she was to give the word to the doctor, but she absolutely refused. I'll never forget what she said that day. 'Jonathan,' she said to me, 'once this child is born, I won't be with you to scold you for leaving your cigars in the study. Tell the child that I love him and always will, as I *hopefully* pass into the Father's arms.' How do you like that? Joking around even though she knew she was going to die. 'If the child happens to be a boy,' she continued, 'call him Bartholomew, after my father. But if it's a girl, God help you!' And that was it. She went into labor and died. She never told me what to name the child if it was a girl, so I named her Rosemary, after her. When I looked down at that beautiful baby girl, I knew to expect mischief. But there cannot be a human being alive who could ever love my Rosemary as I do. Tell her that, Morgan, and also not to blame herself for being unable to sit at my bedside. It is not her fault. I want her to be well and visit my grave when that state finally comes."

Morgan repeated all that Mr. Wheaton desired to be said to Rosemary, watching as Mary's eyes bubbled up with tears. Timothy was hearing all of this for the first time, and could feel Mary's grief. Mary's tears continued to roll as she and Morgan exchanged a final tender embrace.

Mary would have to wait ten more days before she was allowed out of doors. The day when Dolly announced that the fever had gone, and all that remained was a slight cough, overjoyed her immensely. It was clear, at that point, where she would be going first.

Chapter Three

*M*ary was feeling better than she had in months, as she moved down the stairs and into the breakfast room. There, she saw bowls filled with food, and smiled. "You know as well as I, Mr. Sheridan," she said to the cook, "that I cannot eat this all."

"And I wouldn't expect it, Miss," was his reply. "Perhaps you need help."

Seeing some of the servants peek from around the corner, Mary laughed and waved them in. "You are a sneaky one, you are," she said, eyeing the cook, and they all sat down for a meal.

Many of the house servants took their seats at the breakfast table with Mary, first saying grace, before serving themselves. Some of those who partook of this meal had been working at Wheaton Manor since Mr. Wheaton's youth. Though many of them were getting on in years, they still enjoyed working for the family.

Already two minutes into breakfast, enough food had been consumed for the conversation to begin. "Miss Wheaton," one of them spoke up. He was the father of Benny, and a sweet man to be sure. "These past days, you've been called upon at least thrice."

"That's strange," Mary responded, looking suspiciously towards Dolly. "I did not get any word of it at all."

"I took care of it, Miss," Dolly admitted, taking a bite of meat. "You were still not well, and I did not want to bother you with such silly matters."

"Give me the consolation that you didn't write the letters yourself, Dolly," Mary hoped, raising a hand to her head in concern. The nurse snickered, but did not respond.

There was a slight silence. "I wrote them," a young servant girl finally admitted. "You needn't worry."

Relief overcame Mary, and thanking the servant, she continued to eat. "But," the servant continued, "Miss Morgan and her brother have called on you today. Do you wish me to decline?"

"No, no," Mary shook her head. "But I'd rather they come here. I am still indebted to their family for the lovely meal they gave me before my departure to Osiris Creek. I'll write to them directly."

Rising from her seat, she bid the servants good-bye and went to the drawing room to write Morgan. She then gave Benny the letter to deliver, and returned to her chamber. There, she dressed herself for the outside and left Wheaton

Manor. She took a stroll down the roads of remembrance, often being greeted by the townspeople. As she neared the cemetery, the number of people she passed lessened until there were none around.

The air was chilly and the sun blocked by gloomy, gray clouds. She watched as the birds hastened to their nests without offering a single chirp of greeting towards her. The dead leaves fluttered across the streets and the gentle nudges of the wind pushed the naked trees to a gentle rustle. Peering over towards the graveyard, she could feel its coldness icing over her veins, as with each step she drew nearer to it.

The gates were open, but not to the point where they welcomed anyone. Pushing one aside, she heard the creak pierce the ever-disturbing stillness, and looked around. She walked past headstones dating back to the 1600s, and scanned the grounds for any signs of her father's headstone.

A gust of wind suddenly swooped by. She grasped her cape as tightly as she could and turned her back against the wind. Her eyes then came upon what she had been looking for, and she hesitantly tip-toed her way towards her father's headstone.

There it was -- helplessly sitting amongst dead daffodils. She felt sorrow overcome her, and resting a hand on the stone, she gently stroked it, letting her fingers caress the letters of his name and the carved epitaph: 'Jonathan Klaus

Wheaton: 1799-1845. A loving father and devoted servant of God'.

"He was so much more than that," she whispered through her tears. "But what great qualities can be put to words?" She hugged the stone, letting her tears roll upon it, and she spoke to it as if he were right there with her.

"Oh, Father," she went on, drying her eyes, "if I could be half of what you were."

"You're my child, are you not?" Mr. Wheaton said. "Technically you are half of what I am."

"No," she laughed, wiping more tears away, "I mean your qualities. No person can come close to you."

Mr. Wheaton laughed. "Well I certainly hope not!" he responded, quite jolly. "This world has problems enough of its own. My dear Rosemary, wipe away your tears. I live on in your heart and am always with you. Don't cry."

Mary looked up, feeling that her father was with her that instant, and smiled towards the sky. She wiped the remainder of her tears away and stood up, putting a hand to the stone. "I won't," she said to him. "Just for you."

Turning to go home, she was startled when the undertaker came into her line of sight. She was now able to see his features in their entirety. He, indeed, appeared very young and his eyes were as intense as they were the first time she saw them. His solemnity did not leave him and his gaze gave her the impression that it was his custom to stare before he spoke.

"You frightened me, sir," Mary admitted as she composed herself the best she could.

His eyes averted for a moment, as he peered over to her father's headstone. Returning his glance towards her, he said, "I found your horse." Mary stood mute. But he said no more as he motioned her to the stable. She obediently followed, feeling the same awkward sensation consume her just as it had the night she first met him. What he said was true, though, as she found Wilbur happily neighing with the undertaker's horses. Apparently, the man had taken very good care of him, since Wilbur looked brushed and well-fed.

She didn't know what to say, as she petted her horse's muzzle. She was greatly pleased to see the wolves had not killed him, and also pleased that he had been well taken care of.

Her fingers brushed through his mane as she scratched behind his ear, just as he liked. Turning to the undertaker, she plucked up her courage to speak to him. "Thank you, um…" trying to draw him out to reveal his name. He either didn't take the hint, or was too resentful to speak more than was necessary to her. Mary, therefore, was obliged to come right out and ask for his name. "I'm sorry," she said with an uncomfortable smile, "I did not catch your name."

The man studied her, letting his eyes fall down and then back up her figure. They narrowed, as if he suspected her of something. This took her aback, but he eventually opened his mouth to say, "It's Nicholas. Nicholas Black."

"Ah," she said with a lovely smile, "well thank you, Mr. Black. I am very grateful to have met you."

She patted Wilbur as Nicholas released the animal from its stall. Mary was glad to be on her way, but her heart did not feel at rest as she went to exit. Knowing she might regret it later, she turned round and called out to the undertaker. "Mr. Black," she said. He turned, and Mary swallowed her fear. "I have called upon a few friends from town to dine with me this evening. There is always room for another soul, and I would be honored if you could join us."

Mary could hardly believe what she had just said. What would an evening with an undertaker be like, anyway? What would she talk to him about, since he barely spoke in the first place? But she felt she needed to ask, because she considered herself indebted to him. He, after all, did save her life and had tended to her prized animal.

Doing what she could to hide her fear, a weight was lifted from her shoulders when he said, "Very kind of you, but I regret I must decline. I have a coffin to prepare."

"Nobody in town, I hope," Mary found herself saying.

Nicholas glanced at her. "Yes, I'm afraid," he replied simply.

Nicholas then tipped his hat towards her and turned to enter his workshop located at the very back of the cemetery. Secretly, Mary was glad, but at the same time, she deemed herself responsible for a debt.

Not wishing to dwell on this topic any longer, Mary mounted her horse and galloped away to Wheaton Manor. There, the servants took her horse in to its stable, and she prepared for her guests.

Chapter Four

*A*bout six in the afternoon, Rosemary's guests arrived. Morgan was her smiling self, while her brother stood by, listening to both his sister and Mary as they monopolized the conversation. He didn't mind, though, because he knew that they would include him sooner or later. Oftentimes he spoke with Mr. Lou who was very interested in hunting, just as he was. If he had tried that topic on the girls, they would have waved him off and returned to their own interests.

They played a few card games in the parlor as they waited for supper. Here was Timothy's opportunity to speak.

"Today is the first day you've left the house?" he inquired of Mary, tossing down a few cards in the process. Mary nodded.

"Yes," she responded. "I went to visit my father in the cemetery."

"He in good spirits?" Timothy asked, grinning at his attempt at humor. Both the girls glared at him.

"What a horrid joke, Timothy," Morgan replied, slapping a card on the table. "You should know better than to borrow Papa's sense of humor."

"I recall your father as being good-humored," Mary said to her. "I believe your brother resorts to digging up his jokes in the graveyard."

"So that's what the grave robbers are after!" Morgan jestingly concluded. Mary took her mind off the game, and now focused on their discussion.

"Denny's Grove has grave robbers now?" she inquired seriously. "Since when?"

"It's always been occurring," Timothy broke in, raising an eyebrow at his card hand. "It hasn't been until recently that the papers are finally acknowledging it."

"They're mainly after those souls from earlier times," Morgan went on. "Many of them were buried with more gold and jewels than people are these days."

Mary was troubled by this. "That's terrible," she said. "What is the undertaker doing about all of this?" Morgan and Timothy lowered their hands and exchanged glances. They shrugged their shoulders, somewhat hesitant to say a word. It was not like the Greenwoods didn't want to answer the question; it was more of the uneasiness the subject stirred.

"Who knows," Timothy eventually spoke up, laying a card on the table. "No one has ever seen him face-to-face."

Morgan could see that her brother would say no more, and picked up where he had left off. "He shrouds himself within the various buildings on the grounds," she said. "He's such a private individual that many are of the opinion that, perhaps, he's involved in these desecrations."

"Everyone has their right to privacy," Mary replied. "Besides, the business in which he engages himself is not exactly the most uplifting. Perhaps he desires that no one see his sorrow."

"He's been digging graves since his birth," Timothy offered. "If he has any sorrow, it would be lost in his grimness."

The group ceased their conversation for a moment or so as Morgan slapped down the last of her cards. "Gin," she said, delightedly. Timothy threw down his cards and dealt the next hand. They now continued their earlier discussion.

"I admit," Mary spoke up, "he is a little grim, but he is quite gentlemanly." Timothy spewed the cards in shock, startling the girls.

"You saw him?" Tim asked, quite stunned. Mary nodded.

"Yes," she said. "Twice, and I've only been around for a short time."

The siblings looked at one another, not sure what to make of Mary's words. Timothy collected himself and picked up his cards, while Morgan tried to make sense of what Mary had said.

"You must have seen his son," she concluded, now more composed. "He and his son work together in maintaining the grounds. Some of the townspeople call them Death and Nicholas the Grim Reaper's Son. Quite fitting, too, if I do say so."

"Why, because they're undertakers?" Mary asked, laughing. Timothy shook his head.

"No, because it seems that they can tell death days before it even occurs."

A chill came over them. Of course, the entire idea seemed absurd to Mary. How could someone foretell a death days before it had even occurred? She felt it was impossible, and told the Greenwoods that they were exaggerating.

"Oh come on, you two," Mary said, breaking the stillness. "I thought you were above town gossip."

"'Tis no gossip, lass," a voice called out from the door. Turning, the trio saw that it was Mr. Rodchester, the oldest servant in Wheaton Manor. He was a rather hefty fellow, with plump cheeks and gigantic feet that would make loud thuds every time he walked. He was the type of person who would be hiding in some dark alley, ready to tell you a tale, whether you desired to hear it or not. His intense stare made it difficult to leave the room, too. Once a person had entered his realm, there was no turning back.

He advanced on the card table and bowed to them, glaring down at each of them in turn. He raised his head and smacked his lips in a bit of a disturbing way, while he rested his dirty hands on the table. "What yer friens say be true, Miss Rosemary," the man slurred in a heavy Scottish accent. "Cairns Black came to Scotland hundreds o' years ago wi' hi' boy from centra' Asia after bein' driven ou' by the people. As pu'ishmen', he drowned the region wi' the Black Death. From Scotland, he come here and been here eva since. They come to the Grove a few shor' months after ye had gone, Miss Mary. The town co'sidered them as regular folk, but whe' death be at the door, he and the young lad wood fashion coffins tha' fit the stiff just ri' wit' no miscalculatio'. And, whe' someone come abrushin' wi' death, Death play the fiddle, and then they be nothin' but moldy sheep haggis!"

Mr. Rodchester's disturbing tone, paired with his overly animated hand gestures, reduced the table to silence. All three stared at him, both startled and curious, and did not once remove their eyes from him. He was very much into the story, too. He had been a sailor once, and sailors often tell tall and fanciful stories out of the sheer boredom on the seas.

When Mr. Rodchester was done, the room was quiet until one of them finally broke the stillness. "Well thank you for that, Mr. Rodchester," Mary said awkwardly. "That was…I'm not sure what that was."

"It's fact!" the servant cried, raising his hands high over his head. "May ye and the other young lasses of Denny's Grove kno' of Death and hi' son!"

Before anyone could respond to Mr. Rodchester's outlandish tale, Dolly came swooping into the parlor, grabbed the old man by the collar, and scolded him for leaving his room. "You're supposed to be telling stories to the boy, not to Miss Wheaton's company," she informed him with a twinkle in her eye. "Don't you be throwing all this nonsense around about the undertaker and his son."

"Nonsense?!" the man cried, now offended. "Is everythin' I say nothn' to you?"

"Yes," Dolly replied, "Not only this, but it's hogwash! Now off to bed with you."

Grudgingly, the old man consented and grumbled his way out of the room. But before he was gone, he cried out from the door, "Ye be warn'd! Ye be warn'd!"

"They be warn'd!" Dolly shouted back at him, shoving him up the stairs. "Will you get your ars into your room?! Your shouting will wake the neighbors' bairns!"

The old man's objections lasted the entire trip up the stairs and those assembled in the parlor below heard it until the very end. They finally heard a door slam, and then Dolly sigh in relief, "You old coot!"

Mr. Rodchester did the heavy labor around the house. He was the best at it, which may be why everyone put up with his strange behavior. He had turned sixty in the summer, but his heart was built like a twenty-year-old's. Whenever visitors came, though, Dolly was forced to lock him in his room for the safety of the servants and guests. One can only imagine his conversation with Mary and the Greenwoods, had alcohol been added into the equation.

When Dolly returned, the other servants stared at her. "What are you looking at!" she yelled at them. Instantly, they returned to their duties. Mary, on the other hand, was caught between mortification and laughter.

"I am so sorry about that," she apologized to her guests. "I have no excuse to make for him. He's normally like that."

"Oh, we know," Morgan assured her, withholding a chuckle. "I remember the last time we were here, Mr. Rodchester began to fashion my hair and dance with Timothy. It was quite an experience."

"And you tell me this now!" Mary cried, embarrassed. But Morgan and Timothy laughed.

"Why are *you* offended?" he asked. "It's a memory we can all have a good laugh at."

"We're family anyway," Morgan joined in. "We share each other's degradations."

Just then, a servant girl entered the room and bowed, informing them that supper was ready. Overjoyed at the news, Timothy jumped up from his seat and rushed to the dining room. Mary and Morgan, however, took their time, walking together arm-in-arm. "Shall I leave the card tables out, Miss?" the servant girl questioned. Mary nodded.

"Yes," she said. "We shall return to them."

Chapter Five

*E*arly the next morning, Mary fell out of bed and jumped to her feet. She made her way over to the windows and opened the curtains. Looking out, she saw people on the roads carelessly passing the house. It must have been warm, because not one person was wearing a cloak.

Running back to her bed, she threw the strewn covers on top of the other ruffled sheets and flew to her closet, looking for a spring dress that would do for the weather. She ran down the stairs and into the breakfast room.

"Good morning, Dolly," Mary greeted her nurse. "Any news for me today?"

"Not that I know of," the woman answered, setting a plate in front of her. "But that might change just as quickly as the weather, dear." Mary thanked her, and Dolly left to do the laundry.

The day was pleasant, which was rather uncommon, and Mary took advantage of the weather. She went into town and the countryside, greeted by everyone along the way.

She nodded and smiled, noting how very different their attitudes now were towards her. The rich folks paid special attention to her as they drove by in their carriages. The women waved their handkerchiefs, while the men turned to stare and make comments about her. Most women would bask in such attention, but not Mary. It shamed her, while at the same time it annoyed her.

Perhaps she should not have gone into town. But it was a little too late to turn back, now that a certain gentleman had caught sight of her. "Miss Wheaton!" the young man called out to her. She closed her eyes for a moment, then turned around to face him, a bland smile on her face. She knew that voice all too well. His name was Ian Hearn, a man who had liked Mary since he had first laid eyes on her. The problem: he was a very strange individual. He was very attractive, but the way he went about courting ladies was discomforting.

Now approaching Mary, Ian bowed, taking her hand into his own, and kissed it. "I have waited for the moment when I would see you, Miss Mary," he stated. "I called upon you, but I was informed of your sickly state. Oh, to see an angel in such a condition! But I see now that you are looking, if you don't mind my boldness, as captivating as ever." Mary grimaced somewhat, doing what she could to maintain her equanimity. She smiled awkwardly and pulled her hand away from his.

"Ah," she said in a shaky tone, "Mr. Hearn. You never fail to flatter me." She could feel her teeth grinding as she forced these words out. He apparently seemed flattered by the compliment he felt she gave him, this only encouraging him to further his advances.

"You are too kind," he replied, bowing once more towards her, "but I believe your words to be too saintly to be bestowed upon a gent such as myself." She wanted very much to leave, but the instant she moved her foot, he moved his. "What grace you have acquired since your fourteenth year," he went on. "Those who thought you to have already reached your prime and never have more beauty to offer, have surely mistaken themselves."

"I am greatly honored by the compliments which you have bestowed," Mary said, now looking up the road, "but I regret I must return home. There are still some matters which I must settle on my father's account."

"Then you shan't be handling these matters alone!" Ian cried, bowing again towards her. "I shall accompany you home."

"Very kind of you," Mary replied, "but I…"

"Indeed you shan't think of returning home alone," Ian interrupted, toying with his hat. "Such fine beauty would be in danger of falling into the vulgar grasp of murderers and criminals." He was now playing with her hair as he said the word 'beauty'.

Taking a deep breath, Mary removed his hand from her head. Doing what she could not to show her aggravation, she calmly distanced herself from him, saying, "Murderers and criminals mostly come out at night, Mr. Hearn."

He recovered his ground, grabbing her by the hand again, and went on. "Oh, no, no," he insisted, "there are also daytime fiends. Have you not heard? I will not hear of you going home alone."

When Mary felt all hope was lost, she was about to consent until Malcolm Henderson came to her rescue. "Mr. Hearn! There you are!" he cried out from behind the pair. Turning round, they saw a slender, young man approaching them. He had dark, brown hair, neatly groomed and tied in the back by a navy blue ribbon. His eyes were a light blue and he was a strapping man with a contagious smile.

With Malcolm's arrival, Mary sighed in relief, feeling more at ease as he joined in their conversation. "I'm so glad I found you," he said, looking towards Ian. Mr. Hearn appeared to be a bit disturbed by Malcolm's interruption but bowed nonetheless. "Your father," Malcolm went on, "came across that wooden chest of yours."

"The one with the gold lock?" Ian queried, now very much on edge. Malcolm nodded.

"Yes!" he confirmed, trying to contain his laughter. "All sorts of questions are going through his mind. I suggest you settle the matter with him straight away before he burns the box."

Struck with fear, Ian excused himself and ran off in the direction of his home, crying, "Don't burn the box, Father! I can explain!" Once he was out of sight, Malcolm laughed, feeling a bit guilty at his trick, but at the same time grateful that he had freed Mary from Ian's clutches.

She wasn't sure what to make of it, though, and once he had gone, she curiously inquired, "What's in that box that's so important to him anyway?" Malcolm composed himself before he spoke.

"He collects locks of women's hair," he replied, barely holding in his laughter. "Every woman that he meets, he snips off a little piece of their hair and keeps it labeled in a small, wooden box. He even has yours."

"Good Lord!" she cried out in disgust, trying to forget what she had just heard. "I will forever have nightmares!"

"Don't let him bother you," Malcolm said. "He means well. His social skills aren't very refined though, now are they?"

"Just his social skills?" the girl questioned, still shaking her head.

They let the subject drop as it was making both parties somewhat uncomfortable. Mary was grateful that Malcolm had saved her and told him so; he smiled and walked her home. She much preferred his company to Ian Hearn's, and arriving at Wheaton Manor a few minutes later, the two said their good-byes and went their separate ways.

Upon entering the house, Mary found Dolly speaking with Denny's Grove's banker, Mr. Louis Parker. He was short, perhaps even shorter than Mary herself, but his position made up for it. He was sharp when it came to numbers; but with everything else, he was like any regular old man. His steps were slow, he shook as he spoke, and his condition made others think he was on his last legs. But if this was so, he would have been on his last legs for the past twenty-eight years.

Upon hearing the door close, Mr. Parker and Dolly turned around. "Miss Wheaton," he happily declared, putting his suitcase on the ground. "Good to see you again. Look at what a beautiful, young woman you've grown to be!"

"Good day to you, Mr. Parker," Mary curtsied in response. "To what do I owe this pleasure?" Looking around, Mr. Parker picked up his suitcase again and put a hand close to his mouth, whispering to the girl as if the servants were going to steal away with his words.

"I'd rather we speak of this in private," he whispered conspiratorially. The girl smiled slightly, giving her gloves and hat to a servant. She directed the banker into her father's study which had been undisturbed since his death.

She was first to arrive in the room, and turning round to offer the banker a seat, she discovered that he was nowhere in sight. Wondering where he could have gone, she sought him out and found that he was barely past the staircase. Smiling to herself, she returned to the study and waited for about two minutes until he finally arrived.

Another two minutes passed before he sat down and made himself comfortable. She closed the door, watching as he fidgeted with his suitcase and cane, and seated herself next to him, wondering what his coming here could mean.

He was very kind when he spoke. He looked at her with sympathetic eyes, patting her hand gently to reassure her that all was well, or at least would be soon.

"My most sincere condolences, Miss Wheaton," the man spoke in a gentle pitch. "Your father was a very good man. I never met anyone quite like him. When you went off to Osiris Creek for your studies, he and I would play cards together. He always cleaned me out, though. Hmmm…"

Trailing off, the old man comically brushed his hand under Jonathan Wheaton's desk. "No aces," the old man chuckled. "I suppose Lady Luck just preferred him." Mary smiled.

"This old man should get down to it, shouldn't he?" Mr. Parker said somewhat chuckling. He slowly opened his suitcase, searching through the mass of papers that filled its interior, and pulled out a thin, red folder. He set it on the desk and placed his suitcase back on the floor. Waving to Mary, he paused a moment, reaching for his glasses in his vest pocket. Once the glasses had rested on his nose, he read over a few lines of the documents to himself before he spoke.

"Mr. Winkleman is your financial advisor, correct?" Mr. Parker read. Mary nodded.

"Indeed," she responded. "He has been overseeing our assets since my father and mother wed."

"Hmm," the old man mumbled, then sat quietly for a minute, double-checking the clauses in the documents. Mary watched him too, wondering what his coming could mean. Sensing that something was wrong, she questioned him directly on the matter.

"Forgive me," she said, interrupting his train of thought, "but is there something I need to tend to?" Mr. Parker removed his glasses and looked over to her.

"No," he said, "but there is something you should know."

Pushing himself up from his chair, he took a little stroll around the room and peered out the window in thought. "You have no cousins, no uncles, nor any male counterpart," Mr. Parker pointed out. The girl was well aware of this and said so herself.

"Yes, sir," she replied, "unless some distant relative has come forward."

"Oh, no!" Mr. Parker cried, making his way back to his seat, "nothing like that. It's just…your father trusts you so much." The girl held in a laugh.

"Alright," she said, half smiling. "I suppose I see the problem now."

"No problem at all, Miss Wheaton," the banker quickly replied. "It's just so strange that the deceased doesn't leave a trustee for someone as young as you."

"Is this what you wished to inform me about?" Mary asked, wanting to get Mr. Parker to the point before he rambled on. Gradually, the old man shook his head.

"No," he said in a sort of daze. "But your father allows your income to be about five thousand from now on -- that is, unless you marry. In this case, it would be increased by 1500 pounds." Mary shrugged her shoulders.

"Is that bad?" she asked. The banker looked astonished. "Well, no," he responded, "but it is an amount less than you would receive if you wed." Still, Mary saw no issue.

"I don't go on wild spending sprees as many before me have done," the girl firmly stated. "I only spend on what is necessary. Mr. Parker, money is not my concern. I could care less if I was poor, much less rich. You seem to assume that it is the primary concern in my life."

"It is a big concern, Miss Wheaton," Mr. Parker interjected. "What if you lost most of it through..."

"Mr. Parker," the girl gently cut him off, "Money might be others' main concern, but as for *me*, God is mine. Mr. Winkleman is caring for all the taxes and those financial things of which I do not understand. I assure you, everything is handled. I believe I can survive on the funds which my father left me."

To say the least, Mr. Parker was astonished at the girl being so casual. Women in her position would be worrying themselves with all the financials and seeking out a husband to help their situation. The banker was not especially used to people like Mary, but he surely wished there were more like her!

With all this said, Mr. Parker had nothing more that he needed to share. He, therefore, grabbed up his cane and suitcase and went to leave before he remembered something. "I almost forgot, Miss Wheaton," the old man said, working his way slowly back to his chair. Reaching into his pocket, he withdrew a key on a chain. "Your father wanted me to give this to you." He handed the item over to her and she took it with a puzzled look.

"It's a key," she said half to herself and half aloud. "Is it for anything?"

"It must be," he replied simply. Mary shrugged her shoulders.

"Did my father tell you what it was for?" she inquired. The old man shook his head.

"No," replied he. "When he gave it to me, he said, 'Rosemary's a smart girl; she'll figure it out'."

Mary stared at the key for a long while, then hung it around her neck. "I thank you, sir," she replied. "And I wish you a good day."

"Not gonna happen," the old man said in a serious voice. Then a sparkle returned to his eye when he finished by saying, "My wife's home."

He left Wheaton Manor in good spirits and Mary went to her room to read. Mr. Parker had been there long enough for darkness to follow, relinquishing any hopes for another outdoor excursion.

Chapter Six

A month had passed since Mary's arrival at Wheaton Manor and she had already been called upon seven times. The first was Ian Hearn, but she made all the excuses she could to stay away from his residence. He again tried to call upon her after seeing her in town, but she declined on the grounds that she had already made a commitment to meet two women that she had known as a girl. Truth be told, she did not like the girls. They thought highly of themselves mainly because they had money, and those whom they felt were not up to their standards were treated like dirt. Mary felt in no way bound to accept their invitation, but her choices at the time were limited to them or Ian Hearn. Her decision was clear.

Warmly, the two overdressed girls greeted Mary as she walked in. One, named Jane Phillips, was clothed in a purple colored, silk dress, decorated with feathers and gems at the collar and golden lace at the stomach. The second, named Eliza Orchid, wore blue satin and as many golden rings as her dainty fingers could hold. Judging by the way they were dressed, Mary deduced that they had not changed a bit, and might even be worse than when they were children.

Jane often flaunted her body around, showing off her perfect figure as if there were hundreds of gentlemen in the room, while Eliza contented herself in taking a leisurely stroll about the area. Their noses were always in the air, and when they spoke, it was to complain or criticize. They thought their true characters were far from being discovered, but one minute in their presence exposed them completely for who they were.

"Oh, Miss Rosemary," Jane spoke, grabbing Mary's hand as if they'd been friends for years. "It is so good to see you again. I only wish that we were on better terms than death."

"So kind of you to invite me here," Mary civilly replied. "It has most certainly been a great while since I've been in your company."

"Oh to be sure!" Eliza cried. "Why is it that we have not seen each other since childhood?"

"The times! The times!" Jane replied rather dramatically. "They were all too ill for a gathering. But you are here now, and that is what matters most."

Eliza invited Mary to sit down on the sofa. "So I hear your inheritance is quite considerable," Jane spoke in a forward manner. Eliza smiled slyly.

"Oh yes!" she followed. "And such good news it is too! Any husband you desire, you'll have!"

"If love were based primarily upon money," Mary mumbled.

"What was that, dear?" Jane inquired, unable to hear the girl's response.

Quickly, Mary smiled and said, "Oh nothing…you have such a lovely home."

"Yes," Jane conceitedly agreed. "My father has been very generous."

"Perhaps too generous," Eliza pointed out and Jane glared at her.

"Whatever do you mean by that?" she snapped. Eliza smiled.

"I mean what I say," the girl replied. "He had not only you, but your two older sisters. If you were the only child, his entire fortune would have been yours."

Finally comprehending what Eliza meant, Jane's mood turned to gloom.

"Oh," she sighed, putting a hand to her head, "what fortune I could have owned if I had not those two wretched witches to share it with. They both stole my husbands, you know. The first, Gregory Douglas, was the most handsome man in all of Denny's Grove. He was rich, too, which only added to his charm. But my heinous older sister Penelope took him from me with full knowledge that my love was committed to him. She delights in my suffering! And when

I get over the hurt of seeing my sweet Gregory taken from me, another man comes to wipe away the shards of my broken heart. He might not have been as handsome as Gregory, but he most certainly was richer. But what do you think happened?" She paused for dramatic effect, holding her heart for added passion. Mary stared at her, wondering in her mind if Jane was truly serious in what she said. "Susan steals *him* from me!" Jane cried, throwing herself on the sofa arm. "Oh the torment I endured during those past days! But," she said with another shift in emotion, "my consolation came when my father bequeathed the mansion and much of his money to me, right on his death bed. To see the looks on my sisters' faces! Ha! Oh, what a jolly good show it was!"

Now sitting upright, Jane adjusted her ruffled dress and patted her golden curls back into place. Eliza shook her head at the revolting behavior of Jane's sisters, turned her attention out the window, and sat silently in that manner for several long minutes. Mary, on the other hand, stared at the girls in bewilderment, too dumbfounded to form any words.

Coming out of her emotional tirade, Jane let her hand fall upon Mary's and smiled. "We women must bond together when tragedy strikes, though," she said as if that was her reason for narrating her tale. "Now, whenever I feel miserable about myself, I can take my tears to the servants."

Just as she was speaking, three servants entered with trays of deserts and tea, setting them on a table before them. Jane's eye mischievously peered over at them and turning to Mary, she said, "Here, I'll show you precisely what I mean."

She pulled Mary towards the dessert table, sitting her down on one side of the display while she sat at the head. Eliza took her seat directly across from Mary while the servants distributed little saucers to them.

Winking over at Mary, Jane's demeanor switched from contentment to complete dissatisfaction. "Cathy!" she hollered at one of the servants. "What are these?"

"They're crepes, Miss Phillips," the servant patiently replied. Jane made a face of great displeasure, which the servant knew all too well.

"You know I hate crepes, you stupid servant!" she screamed, as she threw the plate on the floor. "Now pick those up and get out of my sight, you worthless wretch!"

Without any utterance of rebellion, the servant did as she was told and bent her old back down to pick up the scattered desserts. Eliza snubbed her nose at the poor woman, holding back her laughter to the best of her ability, leaving Mary absolutely mortified.

The girls thought nothing of it, though, since this was their regular routine. How anyone could stand serving them, let alone be in their sight was a mystery.

When all the servants had exited, the two girls burst out laughing, wiping tears from their eyes, thinking how funny their cruel trick had been. "Oh how we suffer," Jane broke in from her laughter, popping a grape into her mouth. "These servants just don't know how to do anything right."

"Alas!" cried the other. "Is there no one that could save us?!"

The two laughed maniacally again as they shoved food into their mouths. Turning towards Mary, they tried to get her in on all their petty fun. "Miss Rosemary," Eliza spoke through a mouthful of food. "Do you have this much fun with…the help?"

"The help?" Mary disgustedly repeated. Jane's eyes sparkled.

"Yes," she agreed. "Those put on this earth to serve us."

"Serve us?" Mary echoed. The two girls frowned.

"Well don't just sit there and repeat everything we say," Jane smugly retorted. "We want your opinion. Do you suffer like we do?"

As much as Mary wanted to holler at the girls for their wickedness, she thought it would be best if she calmly addressed her point. Perhaps then they might understand her position in the matter.

"Oh yes," she started, putting tea to her lips, "but in a different sense." Delighted to find Mary on their side, Jane was about to speak again when the girl cut her off. "It's such a trial to listen to ungratefulness, selfish pity, and undying voracity," Mary continued.

"Yes! Yes!" Eliza exclaimed. "Now you get it!"

"And," Mary went on, "not to mention the lack of respect for our brothers and sisters with whom we share the same Christian bond." There was a brief silence as Mary took a bite of the fruit set before her. The women watched her, sitting quite perplexed. Eliza was too fixed upon herself to think anything more of it, but Jane sat in suspicion, eyes narrowed.

"What do you mean?" Miss Phillips asked. Mary's eyes sparkled.

"Oh nothing," she casually responded, taking another sip of tea. "Just that you need not travel far to find avarice consume the soul." Still, Jane's suspicion lingered.

"Do you speak of the servants," she asked slowly, "or of some other?"

"Yes," Mary replied with a slight smirk. Jane's head turned Eliza's way, but her friend had not been listening. She, therefore, was forced to drop the topic altogether and brush it off as nothing but silly talk. "Oh they are proud!" Mary thought, as Jane moved on to another subject, and she simply sat and listened for the remainder of the visit.

When it was time to leave, the girls reeled Mary in for an embrace, pushing aside the servants who were in the process of dressing Mary for the outdoor chill. They kissed her on both cheeks and expressed their desire to see her again. "Don't feel like a stranger," Jane said, displaying a phony smile on her face. "We enjoy your company very much."

"Indeed!" Eliza wholeheartedly agreed. "We have such stimulating conversations with you!"

They waved good-bye to Mary with their handkerchiefs, crying out their farewells and wishes for good health, as the carriage made its way to the gate. But as soon as the vehicle was out of sight, they sighed in relief, glad to be rid of their company.

"That was the most grueling two hours of my life!" Jane cried, tossing her handkerchief on the floor. She threw herself on the couch and turned to Eliza. "Such an ugly creature, too!" she continued, laying her head against the cushions. "I hope that brat gets plowed over on one of her walks home. Hopefully that will improve the nasty disease she calls a face."

"Indeed!" Eliza cried in agreement. "Good thing she has that fortune of hers, or else she would surely die an old maid!"

Chapter Seven

When the festivities in town had settled down, Mary prepared herself for bed. She was exhausted from having had to deal with the two rich snobs of Yardley. Her body could barely stand upright, and her eyes struggled to stay open. Dolly assisted her, removing the various items that kept her hair in place, and watched Mary's relief as her brown hair cascaded down her shoulders.

"Oh, Dolly," Mary exclaimed, brushing out her hair, "if only I were the daughter of some beggar in the countryside. Then I wouldn't have to deal with all this nonsense."

"I beg your pardon!" the servant replied.

"Dolly," she said, "you're family. Whether I'm rich or poor, I would have to deal with *your* nonsense."

"Theoretical family does not quite count, Miss," the servant replied. "And besides, my ears don't quite appreciate such cheekiness."

"I'm ready to slice off mine, though," Mary said, placing the brush back on her dresser. She fell back on her bed in exhaustion. Then, sitting up, she peered out the window and gazed to the road below.

Dolly saw the girl's gloom, though Mary often tried to hide it behind a more relaxed persona, and took up a more serious tone. "Miss," she called over to Rosemary. "What troubles you?" The girl's head shifted slightly.

"I know it sounds a bit arrogant," she said, without making eye contact with the maid, "but I feel so empty. It's just...I feel so alone. God has been so good as to give me you, but there's just this longing. I can't quite place it."

"You miss your father," the servant concluded, taking a seat next to the girl. "It's only been a little bit over a month since his passing. Of course you feel empty." Mary sighed.

"How do you cope with being so far away from Mr. Peyton all the time," she inquired. "You're always so happy and optimistic."

Dolly was struck by the question and lowered her head, thoughts jumbling in her mind. Not knowing exactly how to approach the query, she sighed. Mary was sorry for ever asking, but the maid patted her hand and held back her tears. "Don't be fretful, dear," she said to Mary with a sad smile. "Jerome and I still care for each other. I understand why he has to be away from me, though. He has to stay close to his brothers and sisters and care for them, since they have no one else. You see, I work to provide. The times have just not been right to visit one another."

The servant sat silent for a moment or two, drifting into deep thought after her last statement. Breaking herself away from her gloominess, she turned the conversation back towards Mary, not wishing her despair to consume her mistress.

"Let's not worry about me now, though," she said, exhaling a melancholy breath. "I bet I know what might help fill the void." Mary still held to her concern for her nurse, but she went along with what she was saying, so that Dolly could more quickly put her mind on other matters.

"You speak of marriage, don't you?" Mary guessed, walking over to her bedroom window. "Is that what it ultimately comes down to? But I find not the slightest interest in the gentlemen of this town." The maid shrugged her shoulders in thought.

"What about Mr. Ian Hearn?" she suggested, not at all aware that he disturbed Mary greatly. Dolly immediately saw the effects of her words when Mary turned around, clearly showing her offense.

"Surely you jest!" the girl cried out in disgust. "Me married to Mr. Hearn?! The man collects locks of women's hair, for heaven's sake! What happens if I depart upon some business? Will he cuddle up with his box of hairs he has acquired from me and kiss them goodnight every day I am gone?" Dolly was startled.

"What?" she exclaimed in shock, darting her eyes to Mary for answers. The girl calmed down before explaining further.

"I was informed that he engaged himself in such things," she replied. "And even if reports were not true, he frightens me nonetheless. He's too close to you when he speaks, his eyes seem never to follow yours when you speak with him, and, when you're not looking, he smells your hair to detect its scent, in case he needs to locate you later."

"Scientist?" Dolly guessed. Mary rolled her eyes, but nodded.

Dolly, therefore, was obliged to throw that option out of the window. But Denny's Grove was now a larger town. Perhaps there was one suitable gentleman that she could pick out for Mary. Because she'd been away for nearly five years, though, it would be difficult to select someone that she already knew.

Suddenly, as if struck by inspiration, she turned towards Mary and exclaimed, "Mr. Malcolm Henderson! What about him?" Mary's eyes met with hers.

"What about him?" she asked, trailing off. Dolly rose.

"Mr. Henderson is most certainly your type of companion," the nurse said, but Mary shook her head.

"That's all very nice, but he's engaged to Isabella," the girl reminded her. "She is one of the more sensible women around these parts, and such a good friend."

"Oh, but did you not hear!" the servant replied. "Mr. Henderson did ask for Miss Cantwell's hand in marriage and she did accept. But when he departed for the war, she fell into a pit of gloom. The waiting grew too much for her and upon his return, she instantly broke off the engagement and took the offer of another gentleman."

"No," Mary responded, in shock. "He loved her so! Oh, the heartbreak must have been excruciating! And he did not mention a single word of it to me when we met in town."

"Perhaps because the pain *is* so tortuous," Dolly returned. "But he goes on in his smiling manner, speaking to no one of his hurt."

"Poor man!" Mary could not help but say. "I did not think Isabella capable of doing such a thing. But I suppose I understand her position. Still, I wish more fidelity existed in this world."

She sat down on the sill of her window, looking out at the dark streets below, and watched as the trees waved gently in the slight breezes that whirled by. Her mind trailed into oblivion without her realizing it, and Dolly waited, curious as ever to hear what the girl's thoughts were. She knew well that Mary focused on everything but marriage. When she was younger, she would have gentlemen interested in her, to be sure, but it always seemed to be those that she wasn't the slightest bit attracted to. She did what she could to let them down gently, but many of them did not quite take the hint. Maybe this was part of her reason for moving to Osiris Creek for her studies. There, she was immersed in an entirely different society and she enjoyed it; but it was not home.

Suddenly, she was torn away from her thoughts by the loud crack of a whip just outside her window. She peered out, moving her head back and forth to see through the glare, and saw a black hearse. Two dark figures sat in the front seats, traveling rapidly through town. As quickly as they had come, they disappeared around the corner, while curious spectators emerged from their homes to watch.

"What is it?" Dolly asked, making her way towards the window. She had not seen the hearse, but she did see the many inquisitive folks peering down to the street from their windows, some actually emerging from their homes to speak with their curious neighbors. A few shrugged their shoulders, unaware of what was happening.

"We'll most certainly hear of this in the morning," Mary said, retreating from her window.

She brushed past Dolly, walking to her door, and put her hand on the knob. "Dolly," she breathed, "I wish to sleep now." She blew out her lamp, lay down and closed her eyes.

The next morning, there certainly was talk about the previous night's occurrences. Mary woke early and dressed herself for the cool weather. She skipped breakfast and took a stroll into town for a breath of fresh air.

It was so quiet as to be discomfiting. Those people that were outdoors were going about their every day duties but appeared anxious, often glancing towards a certain building.

Many stopped to stare at Mary as she passed by, in a way that almost questioned why she was even there. Mary shrugged and continued walking, stopping abruptly when she saw the black hearse. A group of about four servants were huddled together, watching as a coffin was loaded into the back of the carriage. Moving slightly to the left, Mary could see an older woman sobbing bitterly in the arms of one of her servants, watching as two figures dressed in black closed off the back of the hearse.

Looking closely, Mary could see that the woman was the wife of Mr. Louis Parker, the banker. "How can that be?" Mary thought to herself, remembering that she had just seen him a few weeks ago.

Further examining the scene, Mary saw the two black figures make their way to the front of the hearse. One of them was completely covered from head to toe. He was a tall, skinny man, and his collar was raised as though it were winter already. Jumping up on the farthest side of the hearse, he waited as the other man paused to give directions to one of the servants. Mary stared at the second man closely, observing that the servant trembled as she spoke with him. Unconsciously, Mary began to stare at him.

When the man had finished talking with the girl, he turned and stared at Mary, as if he had known she was watching the entire time. Her heart ceased its pounding for a second, and she saw that it was Nicholas Black. She looked away, feeling his fiery eyes burn themselves in her mind. Out of the corner of her eye, she saw Nicholas as he ended his conversation. He tipped his hat to the servant girl, giving her a bit of reassurance in her situation. Hopping onto the driver's side of the hearse, he drove away without breathing another word.

When the clatter of the horses' hooves had faded, Mary turned and watched an older servant put his arm around Mrs. Parker and lead her back inside her home. The servants followed, struggling to keep their grief under control, and said nothing to one another as they went. Once they were all inside, the buzz of conversation on the street resumed.

"What happened?" one woman inquired of a fruit vendor.

"I don't know," the fruit vendor confessed. "I only woke to Betty Parker's sobbing."

"The banker was murdered!" another voice chimed in. "Mrs. Parker grew concerned when Louis didn't arrive home at his regular time, so she went to investigate."

"Oh no!" the woman and fruit vendor gasped in unison. This only encouraged the citizen to continue.

"Oh yes! Douglas Rolland said he heard a rumble from the inside. He thought Mr. Parker was moving furniture, as he sometimes does, and thought no more of it. He walked on and then, from his peripherals, he saw two men casually exiting the bank."

"Did he see who they were?" the woman frantically inquired. The man shook his head.

"No, it was too dark for him to make out their features."

Any other pieces of information that Mary did not glean in one part of the town, she knew she would gather in another. But as stories often do, they become mangled and distorted, soon evolving into something so ridiculous that the original story is lost entirely. Nonetheless, it was usually the servants that got it right, and it wasn't long before Dolly received word concerning the actual story. Mary listened as the nurse passionately related the details to her, but Mary did not want to hear of it. Mr. Parker was such a nice gentleman that she couldn't fathom who would do such a thing to him. All she could do was to wait and pray that hopefully those responsible would be brought to justice.

Chapter Eight

A day after all the chaos, Morgan called upon Rosemary for a little gathering at their home. Mary was overjoyed to say the least, since she had not seen the entire family since Christmas of 1840, and heartily consented.

The Greenwoods were sweet people with generous hearts, always willing to lend a hand to those in need. Mr. Greenwood, a retired colonel, shared in their generosity, but he was immovable in the sight of wrongdoing. If a person was to do one thing to upset him, they would have lost his respect forever. Mrs. Greenwood, on the other hand, was more forgiving than her husband. Her mild nature allowed her to view things from a totally different perspective. She was willing to give everyone the benefit of the doubt, even if they didn't deserve it, and she rarely had anything ill to say of anyone. Her genteel ways and considerate heart won people over.

When the bell rang at the Greenwood residence, Morgan's younger siblings flew into Rosemary's arms, hugging and kissing her until she was suffocated with their love. "Now, now," Morgan said, shooing her brothers and sisters away, "we don't want to smother her before she even enters the door, now do we?"

"It's Rosemary!" the youngest shouted. "Rosemary's here, Morgan!"

"Yes, yes," Morgan nodded, "I see. Now go help Josephine with the cooking."

Full of joyful animation, the children scurried off into the kitchen to help the cook prepare their meal for the evening. Morgan gave one of the servants Mary's overcoat and bonnet, and pulling Mary into the parlor, they met with Mr. and Mrs. Greenwood.

"Rosemary Wheaton!" Mrs. Greenwood ecstatically cried out, choking the girl with her loving embraces. "So good to see you! How are you, dear? Are you well?"

"Yes, yes," Mary giggled. "I'm fine. But my circulation…I can't breathe!"

"Oh my!" the kind woman exclaimed, as she set Mary down, allowing her breathing to return to normal.

"Barely two minutes through the door and you nearly kill her!" Mr. Greenwood called out to his wife. "I believe that to be a new record!" Grinning, Mary hugged the old colonel.

"The same as always, Colonel Greenwood," she said to him. "Gone on any fishing excursions lately?"

"None that you'd be interested in, Miss Mary," the man replied. "And how is it that I hear you come to Denny's Grove in a sickly state? I'm sure Dolly has already lectured you on the matter, with Mr. Kent's sermon not far behind."

"Actually," Mary said, "Dolly was the only one this time. Mr. Kent has been too preoccupied in the fields. But, I talk too much."

Mary took a seat between Mrs. Greenwood and Morgan, and turning to the older couple, inquired after their health. "Oh," the old woman beamed, "everyone's been quite well -- quite well, indeed. Mr. Greenwood's foot has not been pestering him lately, the children are more helpful than ever, and Timothy just proposed to a fine young lady today!"

"Mom!" the boy objected, covering his face in embarrassment. Mary's eyes suddenly glimmered.

"Timothy," she teased, "you did not tell me you were engaged."

"It happened just a few hours ago," he said, a bit recovered from his mother's forwardness. "Forgive me for not sending word of it to you directly after the happening." Mary snickered.

"Ah," she said with a hint of teasing fun, "so I'm guessing she is the reason for these festivities." Quickly, Mrs. Greenwood interjected in a rather serious tone.

"No, no!" she said with eyes full of concern. "We wanted to see *you*, dear. We just did not expect the young lady to be joining us."

"Her family is coming as well, Mama," Morgan piped up. Mrs. Greenwood nodded her head, now remembering.

"Ah yes!" she recalled. Turning to Mary, she went on to explain. "It's the Quigleys from the Songbird Village. They have four children and, I believe, a son just about your age, Miss Rosemary."

"Mama!" Morgan cried.

"Sorry, sorry!" the mother exclaimed, buttoning her mouth shut. But she could not keep quiet for very long, because she immediately continued with, "Single and young!"

"Mother!" both Morgan and Timothy cried. Mrs. Greenwood giggled like a guilty child and hastened to the kitchen before she landed herself into any more trouble.

It wasn't long before another knock at the door announced the arrival of the Quigleys. Timothy nervously stood by, as his parents warmly welcomed them, eyeing his betrothed once he caught sight of her. He smiled, waiting for the moment when she could leave for the parlor on his arm.

"Mr. and Mrs. Quigley!" Mrs. Greenwood cried out in elation. "So good of you to join us!" Mrs. Quigley scowled, glaring at her most profoundly, and threw her furs into the arms of a waiting servant, peering around the house with a hint of distaste before speaking.

"Mrs. Greenwood," she said in an airy tone. "It is a privilege to be here. Your home is so...quaint." Mr. Greenwood discreetly rolled his eyes, but his wife took no note of it. "These are my children," Mrs. Quigley continued. "Cawley, Julie, Pandora, and Lillian." All the children bowed and curtsied as their names were called out, but remained silent. Julie and Pandora were the youngest of the four, being twelve and fourteen years old respectively. They mimicked much of their mother's behavior, peering around the home as if filth was everywhere. Lillian, whom Timothy had offered his hand to earlier that day, was the second oldest, being twenty. She was a very pretty girl whose character was totally opposite that of her mother's. She delighted in the home's decor, though it was rather old fashioned, complimenting Mrs. Greenwood on certain pieces of furniture and inquiring into their history. Lastly came Cawley Quigley, the oldest sibling. He was five and twenty, not exactly the most handsome man in the world. He appeared greasy and sullen, taking little delight in the present company.

"So good to meet you all!" the old woman cried without losing her smile. "And these are my children: Harris, Edgar, Jillian, Wanda, Timothy you know, Morgan, and Morgan's beautiful friend, Miss Rosemary Wheaton." The children mirrored the motions of the first group, bowing and curtsying yet with more enthusiasm. But when Cawley heard Mary's name called, he turned to her and smiled, nearly losing his balance.

The entire group entered the parlor; Mr. Greenwood and Mr. Quigley started a game of cards, while Mrs. Greenwood and Mrs. Quigley engaged themselves in conversation. The children wanted to dance, so they coaxed Mary to play a piece for them. Timothy and Lillian stood together, while Cawley moved next to Mary at the piano.

"You play very well," Cawley spoke, though Mary had barely touched the piano.

Awkwardly, she smiled, looking up to him in bemusement, and replied, "Thank you, sir, but I have not yet played anything." Cawley uncomfortably shifted his weight.

"Ah, yes," he said, a bit uncomfortably, "but it appears that you are confident in yourself." The girl eyed him for a moment, then began to play. She could sense his nervousness as he stood by her, tapping his fingers on the instrument, wondering what to say next. She felt somewhat sorry for him and trying to be polite, she resolved to say something. She would later regret it.

"Do you play?" she inquired kindly, without moving her eyes from the keys.

Turning to face her, he quickly replied, "I do indeed. I've played since my youth."

"Is that so?" Mary returned, raising her eyebrows. "What do you do for a living?"

"I am a very successful businessman," he smugly replied. "I sell clothing of the finest quality and make at least ten pounds a week! I believe it's my outstanding charm that entices customers to purchase my products." Nearly losing her place in song, Mary struggled to retain her composure so as not to break out laughing. Cawley, on the other hand, was not helping her cause as he only continued.

"Forgive me for being so forward, Miss Wheaton," he said to her, "but I believe you should know who you're dealing with."

"Thank you for the warning," she responded uneasily, and finished her song.

She played a few more tunes without any further interruptions from Cawley. When she stopped, however, he asked for the pleasure of dancing with her. She accepted, switching places with Timothy at the piano, and stood opposite him, calmly waiting for the music to begin.

"Play Promenade, Timothy!" Wanda shouted out to him before his fingers touched the keys.

Moving to face those on the dance floor, Tim asked, "Is that alright with the rest of you?" Ecstatically, the children cried their approval and Mary smiled, relieved by the song choice. Because the dance called for a constant change of partners, her time spent with Cawley would greatly diminish.

"Alright," Tim agreed, dropping his hands from the piano, "but one of you will have to fetch Father's bagpipes." Jerking out of place, Edgar went to fetch the instrument, returning in a matter of minutes. Circling up, Timothy began to play, while Cawley took Mary's hands in his. He guided her throughout the dance, as if she didn't know it herself, then released her to the next partner. This happened to be Pandora, since there weren't enough boys to go around. Though Mary preferred her over her brother, Pandora was a sourpuss through it all. Edgar and Harris were lovely partners, and Morgan was always pleasant to be with, but when Mary's last partner left her, she dreaded the moment she would be forced into Cawley's arms again.

"Did you miss me?" he whispered in her ear. He twirled her out, then back in again. "Don't answer that; I know you did."

Though the dance was not very long, Cawley somehow made it feel like an eternity. He bowed and smiled to Mary once the song had come to a close, and tried to convince Timothy to play another tune, but without success. He, therefore, was obliged to leave Mary and join the card game with his father and Mr. Greenwood.

Once he had left the girl's side, Morgan strolled over to Mary, and sat down with her on a nearby sofa. "How was the young Mr. Quigley?" she asked, seeing the change in her friend's complexion.

"A bit misguided when it comes to flattery," Mary responded, wiping Cawley's grease off her hands.

"I think you're merely being picky," she said to Mary, but Mary shook her head.

"No, I'm not," she sternly replied. "Speak to him yourself and you will see precisely what I mean."

Taking her up on the offer, Morgan went over to converse with Cawley. Unfortunately, he did not pay very much attention to her because he was constantly distracted by Mary. Morgan considered him to simply be a reticent individual and deemed him as so most of the night, until she overheard his egotism at the dinner table. She was surprised, too, by some of the things he said to Mary. One moment he would hail her as the most beautiful girl of his acquaintance and the next he would try to figure out ways to change her 'simple-looking features'. He mocked her intelligence, and continually brought the conversation back to his own great success as a businessman.

"When I get married," he said, directing his eyes deeply into Mary's, "I refuse to have children. Those ungrateful wretches shan't lay a single hand on *my* wealth. But, if for some reason, a child is born, I will send them directly to boarding school when they come of age. I refuse to deal with such nonsense."

While his words obviously bothered Mary, she kept her attention primarily on Timothy and Lillian. She saw how sweet they were together, even in the little things. She hoped Timothy could live up to the standards of his family. After all, Mrs. Quigley seemed to hate everything, including her husband at times. The only subject that caught her interest in the slightest was money. Lillian, on the other hand, was not worried in the least about wealth, and this greatly troubled her mother.

"You don't want to starve, do you?!" she complained to Lillian. "You want him to have a good job, as well as a significant social position!"

"No, Mother," the girl replied coolly. "That's what *you* want. I love Timothy just the way he is, for rich or poor. Those *are* in the wedding vows, you know."

"Women say their vows without really thinking them over," the mother waved off. "Most marry with fortune in mind."

"Oh, but you and Papa are the exception," Lillian pointed out with a smile, "because I *know* you wouldn't just marry Papa for his money." Mrs. Quigley glared at her daughter with dagger-like eyes that could cut clear across a room. But the girl stood her ground. "Mama," she said very calmly, "I'm marrying Timothy."

Shaking her head in disappointment, the mother turned to her younger daughters for comfort in this time of need. "Oh, your foolish sister is blinded by love!" she lamented.

"Promise me girls, that you won't allow your heart to choose what your brain should!"

"Don't worry, Mama," Pandora assured. "*I* would never marry as low as Lilly. How can it be love if you're forced into begging on the streets?"

"Precisely what I told your sister!" Mrs. Quigley cried. "Oh, where did I go wrong?"

She fell back into her seat and began to toy in disgust with the food on her plate. Her husband eyed her without a hint of compassion. Stuffing a piece of broccoli into his mouth, he interjected, "I wish you would inform me of your design to make all our children into silly fools," he said, swallowing. "Perhaps I should warn Lilly directly."

"Oh stop!" his wife crossly replied, hitting him on the arm. "What would the town think if they hear that the Quigleys' father looks upon his children as nothing but silly fools?"

"No," the husband corrected, "I do not find them *all* foolish; merely Cawley, Julie, and Dora." Mrs. Quigley grumbled. "Oh, how you tease me!" she angrily cried. "I see no pleasure in it!"

"Well, you're not in *my* position, so you wouldn't quite understand, now would you?" he quickly retorted, then went back to eating.

Their meal soon came to a close and the children found their interest elsewhere. As the servants cleared the table, the adults returned to the parlor to exchange words.

Morgan and Mary joined Lilly and Timothy in conversation, while Cawley moped with his mother and two sisters. Mr. Quigley and Mr. Greenwood carried on with their card game, soon to be joined by Harris and Edgar.

"Well, it seems that Mama is taking a certain liking to you, Timothy," Lilly smiled at her betrothed. "She can't stop talking about you."

"Are you sure?" he nervously replied. "I could have sworn I saw her go for a knife." Lilly laughed.

"Of course not," she declared, putting her hand in his. "It just takes time for her to warm up to people."

"I can't stand that boy!" Mrs. Quigley complained to her three children. "He's so positive that it sickens me!"

"Not to mention his smile," Julie interrupted. "It's so very eerie. Honestly, no one smiles as much as that unless they're up to something!"

"Perhaps it's best for Lillian to make her own mistakes," the mother sighed, throwing a hand to her head in distress. "Years later, when her sense returns to her, she'll come wailing home to her mother. I'll be there to say to her, 'I told you so,' but also to comfort her by finding the best lawyer I can to annul the marriage on grounds of insanity."

She huffed and puffed until she was tired of fuming, then threw her body onto the sofa, moaning and whining about the pain her daughter had caused her. Her daughters joined in on her grumbling rant, only to be interrupted by Cawley.

"To be fair," he said, "I don't find Timothy to be the most repulsive soul I've been acquainted with." Mrs. Quigley sat up and glared at her son.

"Are you mad?!" she nearly shouted. "Lillian has scraped the bottom of the barrel with this one!" But Pandora put a hand to her mother's arm.

"Oh, Mama," she said, waving her free hand at her brother, "he's just saying that because he likes Miss Wheaton." That comment did not make Mrs. Quigley feel any better.

"Any person who associates with such company cannot have much sense themselves!" she snapped. "That girl is repugnance itself!" Cawley merely smiled and leaned in to his mother.

"Did I forget to mention that Miss Wheaton is the sole heir of Mr. Jonathan Wheaton's fortune?" he deviously confided. "She's worth thousands of pounds, thousands more than Julie and Dora combined."

Mrs. Quigley's frown instantly morphed into a scheming smile, and her eyes sparkled at the thought of Cawley sharing in that great fortune. She knew she'd have to have it; she, therefore, told her son to do whatever it took to get that money.

"I'm already one step ahead of you, Mother," Cawley conceitedly replied. "I've gone and flattered her far more than any man could ever or would ever. I fear she can hardly stand being separated from me for more than a few moments. She tries, but I see her suffer so."

"Good, good!" his mother exclaimed, clasping her hands. "Finally, one of my children is doing what's best for the family!"

Cawley tried his hand at flattery once more, while Mary did her best to stay patient through it all. Mr. Quigley and Mr. Greenwood vowed to finish their card game, and set a time to meet in the Songbird Village, perhaps allowing a few more friends in on the action. Mrs. Quigley and her two youngest daughters were quite ready to leave, nearly forgetting to say good-bye to the Greenwoods when they saw their carriage pull up. They bid their obligatory adieus, however, no matter how excruciating it was for them.

"Good-bye, Lilly," Timothy saluted, kissing the girl's hand. "I hope to see you very soon."

"Indeed," the girl openly blushed. "Perhaps for a walk about Denny's Grove?"

She curtsied to him and he bowed to her; then she went to embrace Morgan. "It was such a pleasure to meet you," the girl sweetly smiled. "I can feel us becoming such close sisters."

She hugged Morgan one last time, and, approaching Mary, she beamed, curtsying to her without losing her smile. "I enjoyed your company very much," the girl asserted. "I hope to repeat this pleasure again."

"As do I," Mary replied and curtsied back to her. Before Lillian left, she turned back to Mary, first ensuring that her family was out of earshot.

"Oh," she said, "and I'm terribly sorry for Cawley's....well, I'm just sorry for Cawley. He can be just a little too persistent."

"You worry yourself," Mary considerately replied. "He caused no trouble at all."

With that, Lillian and her family left the Greenwood home and not long afterwards Mary did the same. She thanked the family for their hospitality and, seeing her carriage approach, expressed her wish to see them all again very soon.

Chapter Nine

A terrible storm had blown in from the south and crept up on the area without any word of warning from the town's sailors or fishermen. Lightning flashed every few seconds and tree branches repeatedly slammed against Mary's window, abruptly waking her from a sound sleep.

It was still pitch black outside when she glanced over at the clock, narrowing her eyes to read the numerals. Just then another flash lit the room; she saw that it was five thirty in the morning.

Knowing there was no possible way she could sleep through such noise, Mary wrapped herself in a silk robe and exited her room. As she walked down the hall, she found Dolly peering out of one of the larger windows of the mansion, along with a group of five or six other servants, their eyes glued to the outside.

"Some storm," Mary spoke from behind. She obviously startled them, for they jumped. Then, settling down somewhat, they bowed towards her before starting a din, with everyone speaking at the same time. Dolly cut through the noise, ordering the other servants to quiet down.

"Hold it!" she cried out over the clamor. Instantly, every individual fell silent. Relief came over the nurse, now that order was restored, and turning towards Mary, she inquired, "Now why are you out of bed?"

"It's not possible to sleep in such noise," Mary replied. "And why do you crowd round the window like that? You'll blind yourselves."

"There's a man, dressed all in black, just walking around out there," Benny told Mary, pointing out the window.

Curiosity got the better of Mary, so she peered out the window herself to see if she could spot what they had seen. The rain was so heavy, though, that it was almost impossible to see five feet in front of her. "I don't see anything," she said, as she moved away from the window. "And by anything, I mean everything!"

"Well, of course, not now!" Mr. Lou cried, shoving everyone aside. "He passed by about two minutes before you came."

"And what a peculiar thing it was, too!" Mrs. Lou broke in. "He was casually walking through the ferocious winds like it was a clear day!"

"Death be on the prowl for a frisch kill!" Mr. Rodchester shouted from behind. All turned to see him standing in the doorway of his room, eyes wide open and clothes caked in dirt. He brushed through his beard with his long fingernails and lurched forward. But before he could go off on another rant, Dolly ordered him to stop.

"Back to bed, Barney!" she said to him. "We don't need any of your tall tales so early in the morning." He opened his mouth to argue with her, but she didn't give him the chance. "Don't you argue with me," she warned him. "Save your stories for another time."

"Very well," Mr. Rodchester declared, disappointed. "I kno' whe' I'm nau' wanted."

He turned towards his room, but then paused. "No struggle fer my sake, eh Miss Rosemary?" he asked. "As a young lass, ye wood defend me whe' Ms. Peyton here break my spirit."

"Don't you play that card with me, Mr. Rodchester," Mary retorted. "I believe I remember you telling me that if a gentleman does not defend his own honor, then I should hold my ground until he does." The servants snickered, but Rodchester took no offense. Rather, he was proud that she had taken his lesson to heart.

"Oh happy day!" the Scot cried in elation, dancing over to Mary. He grabbed her hands and began to twirl her in his great delight. "You still love me, sweet lass!"

He spun her around and hugged and kissed her before departing for his room. Mary smiled, but Dolly was less forgiving. "No more sugar cane for him," she declared once he had left. She then descended the stairs to return to her work. The other servants soon dispersed and either returned to their rooms or to their tasks.

The thunderstorm roared long into the day, forcing Mary to look for some way to amuse herself. She first tried reading, then knitting; but she was anxious and dropped whatever she picked up. She walked around the house to relieve her restlessness, only to find herself more on-edge than ever.

"This won't do," she said to herself, sitting on the landing. The lightning still flashed and she dropped her face into her hands, trying to wipe away the sleepiness from her eyes. A loud bang of thunder, however, caused her to jump up and look down the hall. When the lightning flashed again, it lit up the door to her father's study.

She stared at it for a while. Then she felt a sudden urge to enter the room. The last time that Mary had sat in the study was when she and Mr. Parker were speaking of her father's estate. She had not had a chance to take a good look at his assets, since she was then still very upset. She felt that it couldn't hurt to take a look at the records now; there was no one around to stop her, anyway.

Her eyes fixed on the doorknob, and she slowly made her way to the door. Her feet felt the cold tiles produce goose bumps as the chill surged up her spine. Her hand finally on the knob, she cautiously opened the door, hesitantly peeking in before she entered the room.

The room was dark, and she had only the light from the storm to guide her. She knew this would not do and patting her way through the pitch black, she searched for an alternative source of light. She stumbled for a moment, feeling her way to the oil lamp that stood on her father's desk.

Switching on the light, Mary got a better look at the room. As she looked around, she saw the volumes her father had read and those he had still not gotten to. Notes were pinned everywhere, reminding him of tasks to get to, since his memory was not the best. He even had notes to remind him to take down the other notes.

But the object that Mary desired most to search through was her father's desk. She made her way back to it and began to search in and around it. She could still smell his aftershave as she sat in his chair, laying her head against it as if she was resting on his chest. She gently wiped the desktop with her fingers, opening the drawers and rustling through the hundreds of documents that were stored inside. Most of them were receipts -- nothing particularly exciting. One drawer, however, caught her attention when she shone the light on it. Memories returned as she recalled sneaking into her father's study to explore it as a child. The inside of the drawers hadn't changed much over the years, but she had never been allowed to look inside the bottom drawer.

Without wavering, she reached for the drawer's handle. She could not conceal her disappointment when she found that it would not budge.

Now sitting on the ground, she stared at it, wondering what she could use to open it. "Maybe one of the servants has the key," she thought as she began to toy with her necklace. "Mr. Kent is usually the one with all they keys."

She mentally explored different solutions when a loud crack of thunder startled her. She gripped her necklace, twirling it to calm her nerves. Suddenly, she realized what she was clasping, and rolled her eyes at her own stupidity. "I think Papa just turned over in his grave," she said, as she removed the key from around her neck. Placing it in the keyhole, she had a rush of excitement when she heard a click. The drawer opened.

Peering in, she found a large green box with a note on top. She withdrew it, wiping off the dust, and read the note to herself:

My dearest Rosemary:

If you are reading this, then I have already passed. If you have found this and I'm still alive, then get your meddlesome, little nose out of here and give me back my key! Now then, I've been keeping this for my own sake and ensured that you never saw its contents. But now that I am gone, I think it's time you saw it. I've always told you what a great woman your mother was, but it was difficult for me to put this to words. These are the letters your mother and I exchanged, before, during, and after the war. You will soon come to understand why I didn't want you to see them. I love you, my Little Rose Petal, take care of yourself. Oh, and don't allow Rodchester around any company. You remember what happened the last time!

Love always,
Papa

Kissing the note, the girl whispered, "I love you too, Papa." She tucked the note under the box. Taking in a deep breath, she opened the green box and found a large stack of letters inside. All of them were dated, the oldest from the year 1817. She shuffled through them, stopping every few minutes.

"This is astounding," she smiled, still fingering them. "And how strange is it that my mother dates things with the month first! Americans are very peculiar."

She picked up the first letter and started to read. It was from her father in the hospital, to her mother. Mary had heard that her father had been injured during the war and been hospitalized at St. Sebastian's Infirmary. There, he had met a close friend named Derek Larson, who was ill with the flu. They kept each other company during their stay, and it wasn't long before Derek had suggested that

Jonathan write to this woman he had formerly dated.
Because life was so humdrum in the hospital, Jonathan had
taken him up on the offer, and written to Miss Rosemary
Smith, an American woman recently relocated to the U.K.

1 March 1817
Dear Miss Rosemary Smith:

*It is a great pleasure to write you, Miss. My name is
Jonathan Wheaton, or Lieutenant Wheaton, of the British
military. Recently, I've been injured and am currently
recovering in the infirmary where I met your friend
Corporal Derek Larson. His quirkiness and exceptionally
lively character have lifted my spirits during these days of
confinement. He suggested I write you and, well, here it is!
I wish not to burden you with the thought of writing back,
and I would not expect it since Derek is involved. From
what he told me, you sound remarkably fascinating.
Forgive me, though, young miss. I wish not to sound
presumptuous in my obvious attempt to flatter you. If you
do choose to write back, I will look forward to your reply.*

Respectfully,
Lt. Jonathan Wheaton

"Good Lord, Father!" Mary cried, as tears of laughter
rushed to her eyes. "No wonder you didn't want me to see

these. This was absolutely hilarious! Your wit obviously won Mama over -- there's no doubt about it."

She folded the letter, returning it to its place in the box, then looked for her mother's response and quickly opened it.

March 27th, 1817
Dear Lieutenant Jonathan Wheaton,

I admit I was surprised to receive your letter, Lieutenant Wheaton, let alone hear Derek's name mentioned. To be frank, I'm not exactly sure what to make of it. This is the first letter I've received that's made me almost forget about the war. Quite humorous, coming from an injured Brit. Well, I suppose I should get to it. As you already know, my name is Rosemary Smith. My father and mother are both British, but they moved to America, where I was born. It wasn't until recently that we moved back to our home in London. It's like an entirely different world, living separate from everyone else. I constantly hear the terminology that my parents found pleasure in practicing in the States being used regularly here. I, however, refuse to succumb to the customs or the accent. I am a southerner and will remain so. Perhaps this account has drawn a somewhat clearer picture of who I am, Lieutenant: a stubborn and persistent American woman. Write at your own risk, and don't say I didn't warn you.

Sincerely,
Rosemary Smith

For hours, Mary switched between letters, watching how her mother and father played cat and mouse with each other. She saw how they slowly became intimate, and before too long, most of the sarcasm had been replaced by romance and flattery.

She read and read until the oil in the lamp burned out. She then returned the letters to their places and the green box in the drawer, locking it with her key. Rising from the floor, she exited the study to get dressed. It was already three in the afternoon and the storm had settled to a calm drizzle.

Chapter Ten

A week after the storm, they held Mr. Parker's funeral. Everyone kept their ears open to learn whether anyone had perished during the great rain storm, but as far as they could tell, every citizen was accounted for.

The service was very beautiful. The priest, who was a personal friend of Mr. Parker, said a heartfelt Mass, delivering humorous anecdotes from when they were both young boys. Mrs. Parker was composed through it all, having shed her tears the night before, and looked on with a peaceful smile, sometimes sighing when the priest recounted a story especially dear to her. People flooded the church, while still more waited outside, respectfully making way when the coffin passed between them. Many offered to be pall-bearers as Mrs. Parker, business associate Winkleman, and Father Moliere led the way to the gravesite.

The day was gloomy and the clouds intimidating, though the wind was presently calm. Even if all hell was to break loose and a storm roared through the area, everyone would stand their ground.

Moving silently towards the cemetery, Mary positioned herself within the massive group of people. Every now and then, she would cast her eyes towards the coffin, wanting so badly to know who would go so far as to kill a kind gentleman like Mr. Parker. Perhaps the killer or killers were in the procession. Oh, what an insult that would be! Or maybe the guilty party had chosen not to attend the ceremony. But she had no way of knowing.

Mary walked on with the rest of the congregation in silence and they reached the plot in a few minutes. Peering over, she saw that there was a man standing beside a freshly dug hole. The people crowded on the opposite side of him, staring down into the hole and then at one another. They waited as the priest took his position next to the man, while the rest of the citizens situated themselves around the grave.

Mary, pushing her way through the crowd, was able to find a spot very close to the hole. She watched as the men lowered the coffin inside, with the aid of the mysterious man, who turned out to be Nicholas Black.

"Brothers and sisters in the Lord," Father began, breaking Mary's concentration. "Let us always remember that Louis Parker is with the Creator now, watching over each and every one of us. Do not weep, for as scripture says, we shall rise again on the last day. Now, I believe

Mr. Winkleman has a few words to say about his business associate, Louis."

The crowd parted to allow a tall man through. Mr. Winkleman stood between the priest and Mr. Black, appearing very much distressed as he looked down at the coffin. When he spoke, his voice shook. Holding back tears as best he could, he addressed some heartfelt words to the congregation.

"Louis Parker," the tall man shuddered, "was like the father I never had. He supported me throughout school, making sure that I had my feet planted firmly on the ground, and never expected anything in return. He would play gags on me when I felt especially low, and always poked fun at me until I smiled, which oftentimes was difficult, since I don't smile that much…"

Mary listened closely, feeling her heart touched by each word uttered. She sighed, daydreaming about her own father's death, and took in a few deep breaths, feeling as if this was Jonathan Wheaton's funeral. She personally felt Mr. Winkleman's distress as he trembled with each word, and it cut to her heart.

But courage soon returned as she lifted her eyes again, this time to peek at the undertaker's son. Without any intention of doing so, she found herself staring at him, watching how his face was completely absent of any emotion. His hands were casually joined behind his back, while his eyes stared vacantly into space. She moved her gaze from him, looking back upon Mr. Winkleman, then let her eyes wander back to Nicholas in fascination.

The ceremony soon ended and the crowd chattily dispersed. Mary, however, stood her ground, staring down into the hole where Mr. Parker rested. So many emotions swelled inside her that she was unable to move. Her thoughts strayed from Mr. Parker's life story and her father's, to death and its impact on one's soul. She felt emptiness, and lingered on, deep in thought, for long minutes afterwards. If it were not for Malcolm Henderson, she might still be standing there long after sunset.

"Miss Wheaton," the kind voice called over to her. She turned and curtsied. She tried to hide her sadness which was so evident. The kind gentleman assured her that it was alright to be sad at funerals.

"It's perfectly normal," he remarked. "Even God cried when he got word of Lazarus' death."

"Ah, yes," Mary tried for a smile, "but I feel like all I do *is* cry."

"Well, you have had a rough life," Malcolm comforted. "I don't mean that in a cruel way but in all sincerity." Mary broke a faint smile.

"When are you ever cruel, Mr. Henderson?" she asked with a tender look. "Besides, I think I'm allowing misery to overcome me. My father's probably reprimanding me from heaven for such feelings." But Malcolm only assured her that there was nothing to be ashamed about.

"They're only natural," he said. "Don't beat yourself up so, Miss Wheaton."

He lifted her hand, holding it firmly between his warm palms. She gazed back, not sure how to react, as he continued, "If I could assist you in any way…"

Removing her hand from his, she said, "I thank you, Mr. Henderson. What would I do without you?"

He smiled and offered to see her back to the manor. She politely declined, saying that she wished to stay a while longer to visit her father. "I understand," he replied without losing face, and then departed.

Standing in serious thought, Mary's gaze followed Mr. Henderson until he disappeared behind the rows of headstones and maples. She walked over to her father's gravestone and touched it. Looking at it with a mixture of anxiety and gloom, she whispered, "It feels like an eternity." She stroked the epitaph and fell to her knees in prayer, occasionally letting a tear or two drip on to the stone. "If only you were here with me," she whispered fretfully. "If only, if only."

Chapter Eleven

*M*onths had passed since Mr. Parker's funeral, yet the authorities never found those responsible for his murder. All seemed lost, and the trail ran cold. Mrs. Parker suffered the most from it. She yearned to have Louis with her again and would ache with pain every day that passed without any news. Mr. Winkleman did what he could to relieve her stress and brought her into his home, hoping that he could restore some normalcy into the widow's life.

Though gloom dominated much of the spring season, summer gave way to new hopes. There was a ball thrown at least once a week, whether it was private or public, and the town soon returned to its regular, buoyant character. Gossip bubbled up from the depths and helped entertain those women who had nothing better to do.

With flowers in bloom, and trees finely clothed with their leafy exteriors, the warm air swooped in and enticed the citizens of Denny's Grove to emerge from their homes and bask in the glory of the season. Carriages now more frequently rambled down the dirt and cobblestone roads, and the clip-clop of the horses' hooves sang children's lullabies by night. Indeed, the town had returned to its people and they were more than pleased to have it back.

Jane Phillips and her snobbish ally Eliza Orchid finally got their time to spread more meaningless rumors around the Grove, savoring the moments when their stories would unearth more delicious tales for them to circulate. The Quigleys, who greatly despised the Greenwoods, watched in horror as Lillian and Timothy exchanged their vows at the altar in early May. The elder Mr. Quigley was thrilled that he now had a son with a good head on his shoulders, much unlike his own son. He shared this feeling with Timothy over fishing or a good game of cards. As for Cawley, he allowed himself to offer praise to the various ladies he endeavored to secure. This is not to say that Mary wasn't uppermost in his thoughts. If he saw her, he was more than willing to drop his wooing of one lady to run after Mary and try his luck with her.

Ian Hearn lurked about Denny's Grove with his wooden box close to him, always keeping on guard for Mary. On the days he didn't see her, he would conceal his wooden box in a leather satchel, harvesting the hair of young women when they weren't looking. If the town ever learned of his ways, they would surely have him locked up for lunacy.

Mary was smart and kept her distance from both of them, giving her time to think, and air enough to breathe. Most of the village bachelors tired of constantly running after her, but they did keep her in the back of their minds in case she happened to appear in town. Basically, she spent her time reading her mother's and father's letters or taking a stroll away from town when the weather was pleasant. She fancied her time alone, but when she became too lonely, she would either turn to her friend Morgan or her nurse Dolly for comfort.

She accepted no invitations to balls during the spring, though she was offered a few, but started to accept them once summer arrived. Most of the dances she did attend were public; and though she despised them greatly, wondering why she ever went in the first place, she still showed up at the next. Every gentleman would have his turn, even those who had barely entered adulthood, and she didn't mind it at all, as long as they didn't court her.

But if there was one gentleman she didn't mind flattering, that would most certainly have to be Malcolm Henderson. She very much savored her time with him. He never had a nasty thing to say about anyone, though there was plenty to go around, and he stayed optimistic, putting aside any thoughts of negativity, if any existed.

As she moved her way through the jolly crowd, she was elated upon seeing Malcolm. He spotted her at the same moment, and, working his way towards her, he bowed, inquiring if she would do him the honor of dancing with him. "Of course," Mary happily replied with a gleam in her eye. "Nothing would make me happier."

He took her hand, dancing the fourth, fifth, and sixth together, while engaging in stimulating conversation. "You look well," Malcolm observed. "It has been a good while since I've had the honor of dancing with you."

"I thank you, sir," Mary responded in just the same attitude. "And I must agree with the interval; it has been too long."

After one dance had ended and another began, the two resumed their conversation. "Where have you hidden these past months?" he continued. "Hiding from the town?"

"I suppose you can look at it that way," the girl laughingly replied. "But perhaps it's not the town I hide from. Perhaps you are the culprit, Mr. Henderson." Malcolm chuckled.

"Oh, indeed what a bad sport I've been!" he cried sarcastically. "Can you forgive such a wretched soul?"

"I believe I shall try," Mary responded, "but the repair will be such an arduous task!"

As she spoke, Mr. Henderson's smile grew in its intensity; that is, until he spotted his former fiancé not far from where he and Mary were dancing. He stopped dead in his tracks, nearly disrupting the flow of the dance. Then his eyes met Isabella's. Mary was quite oblivious to all of this for a moment or so until she noticed Malcolm's strange behavior. She discovered the reason for it approaching them once their dance ended.

Isabella appeared flushed to see Malcolm, but she curtsied, as was her custom. "Mr. Henderson! Miss Wheaton!" she cried out to them. "This certainly is a surprise to see you!"

"And you, too," Malcolm nervously replied, bowing towards the lady. Isabella forced a smile and pulled on her current fiancé's arm, clearing her throat before she continued.

"This is Howard York," she said to them, "my fiancé." The sting of those words reached Malcolm's ears, but he was kind and bowed to him, exchanging a handshake.

"How do you do?" he greeted him.

Isabella awkwardly smiled and turned to Mary inquiring, "Miss Wheaton, how do you fare?"

"I'm well," the girl replied, a little hesitantly. Isabella's eyes curved in compassion, sensing Mary's pain.

"Oh, dear," she said in a softer tone, "I am so very sorry about your father. Was the funeral pleasant?"

"I'm afraid I was too ill to make it," Mary replied, unconsciously fingering her dress. "But I was told it was very pleasant." There was a slight pause. "I hear you and Mr. York are engaged," Mary found herself saying. "Do you have a date set?"

"June thirtieth," Isabella replied. "Mr. York and I are ecstatic." The group then fell silent once more.

Isabella looked around, but Malcolm never removed his eyes from her. He stood silently, even though his heart hurt from its pounding every time she spoke. He wished that she would soon be on her way, and eventually she did leave. The pain, however, lingered on long after she had departed.

Once the other couple had gone, Malcolm did what he could to regain his composure, and assumed a smile. Mary, however, saw directly through it.

"Mr. Henderson," she said, "I think I'm going to return home."

"Let me walk you there," he replied quickly. "I do not wish for you to travel alone."

Nodding, Mary turned, and the two went out into the cool night to return to Wheaton Manor. During their walk, Malcolm said nothing. His eyes were before him and his thoughts in disarray as they strolled on, but Mary was calm as she carefully formed her words. She could see directly through his mask, and could almost experience the hurt he was enduring. Taking a deep breath before she spoke again, she prayed to God that her words would better Malcolm's position.

"The stars are very beautiful tonight," the girl observed, peering up to the skies. Turning slightly, she eyed Malcolm, watching as his shoulders slumped and his face revealed his heartbreak.

He responded, nonetheless, casually thrusting his hands into his pockets, and said to her in a kind tone, "Yes, very beautiful." His words trailed off, and Mary took in another breath.

"Of course, what are they if you've already basked in their glory long before the mere mention of the topic?" she questioned. Here, Malcolm's brow furrowed in confusion and he paused, wondering exactly what Mary meant by this.

"I'm sorry," he said, "but I do not follow." The girl nodded.

"And I do not expect you to," she replied. "Love often blinds the soul." Now Malcolm came to a complete stop, very much startled by Mary's boldness. He turned his head towards town, before returning his gaze to her.

"You're beautiful, Miss Mary, to be sure, but I cannot say that I..."

"Oh, no, no, no," the girl cut him off, "I don't mean me; I mean Miss Cantwell. Will you stop trying to deceive yourself and go and tell her how you feel?" Startled out of his confusion, and striving to hide his emotions, he attempted to tell Mary how she was mistaken.

"Miss Wheaton," the man said, "I don't know what you're talking about."

"Oh, don't you?" she asked disbelievingly. "Well, perhaps I can convince you with these words: Mr. York and Miss Cantwell will be married in a few short days.

That means that time is escaping you. If you don't speak up and inform her that you still have feelings for her, you'll have to go through the excruciating pain of watching her go from being Miss Isabella Cantwell to Mrs. Howard York. Is that what you want?"

Malcolm was now at a loss for words. He hadn't realized that his feelings for Isabella were all that noticeable. Though in his heart, he knew he loved her, yet he struggled against the thought, trying again and again to deny it. But in the end, he knew that Mary was right.

He began to walk again, contemplating the girl's words very intently, and let out a sigh, in a way berating himself for his foolishness. He stopped and turned to Mary, grabbing hold of one of her hands, and wholeheartedly declared as he gazed into her eyes, "You are my liberator, Miss Mary. I would have continued to imprison myself in doubt and pessimism if it were not for you."

Mary placed her hand atop his and exhaled, "Finally! You see the light!"

Peering up, the two saw the lights of Wheaton Manor a short distance away, and strolled on towards them. As they reached the front gate, Malcolm took Mary's hands in his and expressed his deep gratitude towards her. He kissed her on the cheek, patting her hands ever so lightly, and peacefully smiled, saying, "Thank you, Mary. Thank you so very much."

He bowed to her, giving her one last smile before he turned and left, knowing full well what he would do next. She watched as he disappeared into the night, sighing in relief that she was no longer trapped in the middle of this love triangle. She allowed the soft sound of the moonlit breeze to drift over her, and carry her senses away with it. Moving through the gate, Mary took one last glance at the stars before entering her home. "Malcolm is too kind of a soul to be tormented for nothing," she thought to herself, once inside. "If anyone deserves happiness, it would undeniably be him."

Chapter Twelve

"*I*t feels so good to get away from the house," Morgan said as she and Mary made their way to the Songbird Village. "How my brother ever secured Lillian is beyond me."

"That's what every sister says about her brother, I'm sure," Mary replied, fingering her gloves. "It's universal, I suppose."

"Oh, but someone as beautiful and interesting as Lillian?" Morgan responded. "This just goes to show that there is a God after all!"

The girls had awakened early that morning to get a head start to Timothy's home in the Songbird Village. Originally, the two were going to leave by carriage, but seeing how beautiful the weather was, they rejected that idea, much preferring to walk, instead.

And indeed, it was a wonderful day. Children were playing their street games amongst all the carriages and passing folk. They laughed and screamed as they ran deeper into Denny's Grove, meeting up with other children of the village. Clouds were absent from the azure sky, and the gentle breeze shook the trees to wave their greetings to passersby. If only they could be blessed with more days like this.

Mary and Morgan walked through the joyful throngs and arrived shortly in the Songbird Village. They had been deep in conversation, and soon discovered that they were already approaching Timothy's home. They exchanged a laugh before knocking.

Hearing a rustle inside, the girls were shortly greeted by Lillian. "Morgan! Rosemary! You made it!" she called out, embracing both girls so tightly that they gasped for air. She then grabbed their hands and led them to her husband.

"Timothy!" Lilly called out to him. "Our guests have arrived!" Looking up from his paper, Timothy immediately opened his arms to his sister, and bowed towards Rosemary.

"You're a little early, aren't you?" Timothy teased. Morgan gently swatted him.

"Oh, stop," she said. "We'll leave sooner than later, then."

"Oh, Tim," Lillian said, "stop teasing your sister." Turning towards the girls, she continued. "Come, come, girls! Can I get you anything?" Both Mary and Morgan shook their heads. But Lillian insisted on offering them something to drink since they had walked so long. Still, the girls held their ground and sat down.

Lillian joined them, barely able to conceal her excitement, making both Mary and Morgan wonder why she was acting so. She began to rock back and forth, twiddling her thumbs, and humming a little tune to herself, glancing over at her husband as she did so. He sat motionless for a moment or so, ignoring her in order to get her riled up, until he could see that his wife was aching with impatience. "I see you're dying to tell them, Lilly," he finally spoke up, seeing that his wife's eagerness would not be subdued. "Just tell them." Delightedly, Lillian jumped up and walked over to her husband. She placed her hands upon his shoulders, smiling bigger than she had ever smiled before.

"I am so very happy!" she cried without much hesitation. Laying her chin atop her husband's head, her eyes rolled in elation as she said, "Something wonderful has happened; can you guess?" The girls shook their heads. "Oh, come now," Lillian beseeched. "You must guess!" Shrugging their shoulders and exchanging glances with one another, the girls did as they were instructed.

"I bet I know," Morgan piped up. "The Quigleys are moving away!" Timothy smiled and threw back his head.

"Ha!" he laughed. "Don't tease me." Lillian hit him.

"No," she said, "that's not it."

"Oh."

"Is Cawley getting married?" Mary offered. Lillian shook her head again, then stopped.

"Perhaps he is," she admitted, "but that's not it."

"Really?" Mary replied, still dwelling on her previous question. "Who is he planning to marry?"

"Some lady from Yardley," Lillian offered, "but getting back to what I was talking about: something wonderful has happened. God has greatly blessed us, and well, I'm expecting!"

Absolutely thrilled, Morgan jumped up and congratulated her sister-in-law. "How wonderful, Lilly!" she cried, giving her a tender embrace. "When did you find out?"

"Just last week," Lillian replied. "I felt very ill and Timothy called upon Dr. Eastworthy to see what was the matter. He looked at me for a bit, checking my pulse and the like, and set down his instruments after just two minutes. I asked the doctor if everything was alright and he just smiled and said, 'Oh, most certainly is, Mrs. Greenwood! You're expecting!' I was shocked, and poor Timothy looked like he was about to faint. However, he regained his equanimity long enough to ask if he was sure. He said, 'Yes, 100%.' And that's how it happened!"

"More or less," Timothy added, with a smile.

Overjoyed at the tremendous news, Morgan and Lillian spoke about the baby for half an hour more, while Mary and Timothy moved away so that they could speak privately. It had been a good while since Mary had had the opportunity to speak with Timothy, but now that they were together, she didn't know what to say. He was first to speak up, though, noticing that she was suddenly silent.

"How are you feeling?" he inquired with concern. Mary glanced up.

"Very well, thank you," she replied. Timothy could see that something was amiss.

Eyeing her suspiciously, he said, "As Dolly would say, 'That's a load of hogwash'! I *know* something is bothering you, Mary. What is it?"

The girl's eyes met Tim's, then she turned them away in confusion. She knew it was nearly impossible to hide anything from him. "I suppose I'm still upset about my father," she admitted with a heavy sigh. "Mr. Parker's death greatly troubled me, and life at Denny's Grove is just not the same."

"You want to return to Osiris Creek, don't you," Timothy guessed, and Mary looked up.

"You gathered all that from my simple reaction to your statement?" she asked.

The boy rolled his shoulders. "Come now, Mary," he said, putting his hand on hers. "We've been friends ever since we were young children. Of course I can tell if something bothers you. Is it not the same for me as well?" Slowly, she nodded and he went on. "I'm not saying you should remain in Denny's Grove," he resumed, "but I am asking you to really think this over. It is a big decision and you tend to act rashly when faced with such situations."

Lowering her head, the girl nodded, knowing he was right. She would only be fleeing to Osiris Creek to get away from the pain. But the Grove was her home, where all her friends resided. The Wellingtons were fine folk; but other than the one family, the Creek's residents held no special place in her heart.

She sat in deep thought for several minutes and flinched when Timothy called her back to reality. "Are you alright, Mary?" he soothingly asked. She turned to face him, and nodded slightly.

"Yes, yes," she responded. "I was just thinking about what you told me, and you're right. If I am to leave the Grove now, I should be extra sure that that is what I want."

Timothy sighed, seeing Mary still lost within herself, and slid closer to his seat's edge. "Look," he said in a whisper, "you don't realize it, but you bring joy wherever you go, Mary. Your heart and your charming qualities are easy to win people over. Whatever you choose, we will all support you. Don't fret; you'll make the right choice."

He gently kissed her on the head and strolled over to his wife and Morgan. Doubt clouded Mary's perceptions, thwarting any hopes for a quick resolution to her problem. Rising up, she joined the others at the table and listened to their conversation for the rest of her visit.

When lunch was done, Mary and Morgan wished Timothy and Lillian good health, and returned to Denny's Grove. Though the visit was brief, it had been long enough for Lillian to break the news she had been dying to, and get it out of her system.

"Can you imagine?" Morgan said, still excited about having a niece or nephew soon. "I'm going to be an aunt!"

"I try not to," Mary replied. "The poor child needs to be kept from corruption."

"Oh, you tease!" Morgan said. "If anyone corrupts the child, it would be my brother. I hope it is exactly as he was when he was a child."

Now passing the halfway point to their town, Mary's attention wandered over towards the graveyard. She saw her father's gravestone, the flowers already dying, and almost lost herself in a trance. She had been replacing the graveside flowers every two weeks. She found that it was getting to be that time again. Just then Morgan called her name, and her mind returned to the present.

"Mary," Morgan called out to her, "are you alright?" Breaking out of her spell, Mary blinked, nearly stumbling over her feet.

"I'm fine," she replied, regaining her balance. "Sorry, my mind was in a bit of disarray." Morgan paused.

"Are you sure you're alright?" she asked, somewhat skeptical of her friend's reply. But Mary stood her ground, saying that everything was just fine.

"Why wouldn't I be?" she asked. Morgan shrugged her shoulders.

"I don't know," she confessed. "You were speaking rather seriously to my brother earlier. What were you two talking about anyway?" Mary shook her head.

"I need time to think," she murmured. "That's all." Her attention was diverted for a moment when she saw the elder Mr. Black and his son working in the graveyard. She walked on in silence for a few moments before saying, "I really don't want to talk about this now, Morgan."

"And I won't force you," her friend replied, being considerate. "But know that my ears are always open to listen."

Reaching the fork in the road that separated the two residences, they wished each other well and returned to their respective homes. Once inside Wheaton Manor, Mary rubbed her forehead in relief, then ascended the stairs to her room. It was about two thirty in the afternoon.

Chapter Thirteen

*L*ater, as night fell, Mary strolled into town to meet with Isabella Cantwell who had called upon her after her return from the Songbird Village. She had not been expecting this, and felt quite hesitant as she consented to the meeting.

Before Mary's return to Denny's Grove, both girls had been very close friends. They had laughed and played as children; but as the years went on, they grew further and further apart. Mary grew closer to Morgan, while Isabella bonded with other children. Every now and then, they would run into one another and have the best times of their lives. All the festivities ceased once Mary moved to Osiris Creek for her studies at the Wellington home. Somehow, the girls' relationship remained intact so that they could comfortably discuss any topic.

As Mary walked through all the hustle and bustle of the nighttime crowds, she found the restaurant in which Isabella wished to meet. When she entered, a servant greeted her and inquired if she was Rosemary Wheaton. "I am she," Mary concurred, and he took her to Isabella straight away.

When she had gone through a series of doors and hallways, Mary found Isabella in a private room, sitting in a chair by the fire.

"Miss Rosemary Wheaton," the servant announced her, and closed the door behind them.

Isabella's eyes met Mary's and she sprang towards her friend, tenderly embracing her as she cried, "Oh Mary! It is so good to see you! Thank you so much for coming."

"Of course," Mary replied, a bit puzzled.

Sitting down, she adjusted herself near the fire, since it was a bit chilly, and peered over at Isabella, who appeared quite anxious. Mary, too, was anxious to find out why she had been invited, and wasted no time as she inquired, "Are you alright, Isabella? Your letter said it was urgent and I…"

"It *is* urgent," Isabella interrupted. She casted her eyes around for a moment before she went on. "I am so confused, Mary," she replied. "I needed a friend to talk to, and I could think of no one better." Mary lifted her eyes.

"What is it?" she asked, full of concern. "What's wrong?" Isabella hesitated.

"You know that Mr. York and I are to wed very soon, right?" she said. Mary slowly nodded.

"Yes," she responded. "I'm well aware."

"Well," Isabella continued, "I thought that I had my priorities straight when I accepted his hand, but now Mr. Henderson has told me that *he* loves me, and has begged me not to marry Mr. York."

Mary's eyes opened wide. Isabella nodded, rose from her seat, and started to pace the room anxiously. "He told me that he never stopped loving me when I stopped loving him," she said. "Do you know how those words cut into me?! 'When I stopped loving him'? I never did stop! When he went off to war, I constantly wrote to him. I distinctly expressed my love in every note, without fail."

Pausing to wipe a few tears, Isabella sat down. She raised a handkerchief to her eyes, and sobbed again, finding relief in Mary's embrace.

Though confused by the developments between Isabella and Malcolm, Mary waited, comforting her friend as she dabbed her eyes and nose. She must have been holding in all these emotions, with no one to share them with. That was a torment in itself, as Mary well knew.

Releasing her friend, Isabella wiped the last of her tears and composed herself as best she could. "Help me to understand," Mary said. "How is it that you became engaged to Mr. York when you loved Malcolm?" Isabella exhaled.

"It's really my fault," she confessed. "You see, I was told that Mr. Henderson was writing to another young lady in Rothbury by the name of Frances Janus. I waved it off at first, but the reports continued to trickle in, so I confronted the lady who had given me this information. She told me that the messenger came through Denny's Grove at precisely 2:30 p.m. each day, delivering mail to all families of the military. I, therefore, met the messenger the next day at the town's perimeter and told him I was Miss Janus's servant. I said that she had sent me to retrieve any letters at that very spot since business had called her to the Grove.

"He questioned nothing and in about three days' time, I found what I was looking for: a letter addressed to Miss Frances Janus from Corporal Henderson. That was all the proof I needed, and I was determined to forget Malcolm. It wasn't until last night that I learned the truth."

"What's that?" Mary said.

Isabella sighed and replied, "There is more than one Corporal Henderson in the army." Mary tilted her head.

"Well," she said, after an awkward pause, "'Henderson' is a very common last name." Guiltily, Isabella agreed.

Again, she rose in distress and paced the room while Mary stayed calmly seated. She stopped to bite at her fingernails, paced the room some more, then repeated the process.

Mary could understand Isabella's predicament and felt badly for her. But her constant movement now made Mary restless, too. Holding her hands before her, she requested,

"Please stop pacing the room like that; you're driving *me* insane." Isabella stopped instantly and apologized.

"Sorry," she said. "I just don't know what to do now. I love Mr. York, but I love Mr. Henderson, too. What do you think I should do, Mary?"

For a moment, Mary was deep in thought, carefully mulling over the situation. Her eyes would occasionally peek over at Isabella to check up on her condition, but for the most part, Mary was lost in contemplation. Admittedly, she had feelings for Malcolm too, but she knew it would not do, since his heart would always be yearning for Isabella. She, therefore, was obliged to forget her own feelings and step into Isabella's shoes to see what she could do to help.

After a minute, Mary sprang to her feet and guided Isabella back to the table. She calmed her nerves and waited until she was serene enough to listen. Swallowing hard, Mary presented her thoughts.

"Here's Mr. York over here," Mary motioned with her hands, "and here is Mr. Henderson. You're caught in the middle. Now try to imagine your life with either. Think: whom would you be most pleased spending the rest of your life with?"

As Isabella mentally studied both options, the room was utterly still. Not a sound penetrated the walls, except for the clip-clops of the horses' hooves on the street outside. Isabella sat stiffly, with eyes staring before her, intensely imagining what life would be like with each man by her side. Mary was patient and Isabella slow in her choice, but when the bewildered spirit blinked, Mary hoped that she had made her choice.

"It was never a difficult decision for me," Isabella finally declared after a long silence. "I've always loved Malcolm. Perhaps the reason why I was so hesitant in deciding was because I was afraid of hurting Mr. York."

"Feelings will be hurt," Mary said, "but you can't drag Mr. York along if you have no love for him. That's not fair to him. By breaking off the engagement and marrying Mr. Henderson, you'll be doing Mr. York, as well as yourself, a favor."

Peace came over Isabella when she heard this. Deep down, she had known the answer all along; she just needed support from a friend to make sure that she wouldn't later regret her decision. And Mary, seeing her tranquility, was now at ease herself.

Rising up, Isabella gratefully thanked Mary for her patience and advice, and invited her to dine with her sometime soon. "I must go and tell Malcolm my feelings," she said with a relieved smile. "When he told me he loved me, I couldn't respond the way I wished, because of Mr. York. Oh Howard! Now I have to break your heart! The poor thing is already so fragile."

"But it's for the best," Mary reminded. "It's impossible to please everyone."

Isabella nodded, embracing Mary in gratitude, and bid the girl farewell as she went off to find Malcolm. "Glad I could help," Mary offered, and followed her out soon after.

It was ten at night when Mary left the restaurant and began her journey home. She was not accustomed to walking at night, and knew it could be very dangerous. Peering to her left, she saw drunkards and drinkers making merriment of their time; to her right, townsfolk talked amongst themselves, then paused to glare at her as she passed by.

Mary avoided them all, when suddenly a hand reached out from one of the alleyways and grabbed her; she jumped in a panic. "There be none of that, lass!" the voice called out to her, and emerging from the shadows was Mr. Rodchester, apparently in his own element. Strangely enough, in the dark, he didn't appear as scary as he did in daylight.

Releasing Miss Wheaton, Mr. Rodchester continued, keeping an eye out for any unwanted ears in the process. "Wha' ye be doin' amblin' the streets alone?" he asked, scrunching one of his eyes to a close. "Denny's Grove be not the same by day as she be by night."

"Perhaps so," Mary responded, "but there are enough witnesses around if a criminal or murderer should happen to be upon us."

"You're daft!" Mr. Rodchester cried out. "Do yer ears not hear tha'?"

Mary stared at him quite puzzled, but listened to the sounds of the town as she was directed.

Laughter, music, and a few screams were some of the sounds that she heard, but since she wasn't sure what Mr. Rodchester meant, she shook her head and replied, "I don't know what you mean." The Scot appeared surprised.

"Do ye not hear tha'?!" he repeated again. "Listen closely, lass. It be the soun's of a fiddle! Death is playin' his tune!" Mary's brow crinkled.

"How can you even hear that amid all the other noises?" she asked.

Mr. Rodchester stopped, feeling paranoid for a moment, and scanned the streets as the people passed, before he said, "The fiddle tha' Death plays can pierce through any soun'. Death is closin' in! Watch yourself, Miss Wheaton; be on yer guard!"

Mary listened skeptically, rolling her eyes. She put a hand to Mr. Rodchester's shoulder, assuring him that everything was going to be alright. Sadly, the Scot drooped his shoulders and shook his head, disappointed that Mary still clung to her disbelief. "I be a crazy fool then," he said in a gloomy tone. "I waste yer time; forgive me. But I wish to warn anyone who wood listen." Mary sighed.

"I thank you for your warning, Mr. Rodchester," she said to him reassuringly. "I will take all that you have said into account as I go about my way."

Leaving him to tell his stories to another soul, Mary finished her journey through town, first glancing back toward her servant to make sure she hadn't left him in a state of despair. When she saw him, he was already telling stories to Mr. Fackleman, Mr. Winkleman, and Mr. Rolland. Whether they delighted in his tales or not, she was not sure. Rather, she exited the nighttime fever, strolling through the quiet countryside, stopping for a moment when she heard the sounds of a fiddle rise from the graveyard.

Chapter Fourteen

*E*arly the next day, Mary ventured out to the graveyard to replace the flowers at her father's grave. She returned home within the hour, and was greeted by Dolly as she entered Wheaton Manor. Barely was she able to extend her greetings, when the nurse tossed her a letter. "Good morning to you, too," Mary replied to this strange gesture.

Setting her things aside, Mary sat down on the landing, ready to open the letter, when she stopped to examine it more closely. "Dolly," she said, "did you open this?"

Shocked at such an accusation, the maid held a hand to her heart and exclaimed, "I am offended that you would charge me with such a thing," she replied, feeling hurt. "I would never do the mistress such a dishonor." Mary went for the seal again, yet she doubted Dolly's words.

"Is it urgent?" she asked her. The nurse shrugged her shoulders.

"No one shall know until you open it, Miss," she said simply.

Casting her eyes to the letter, Mary opened it. Searching for the sender's name in the upper left hand corner of the letter, she soon discovered that it was a wedding invitation from Cawley Quigley and Jane Phillips.

She lowered the letter. To be fair, the two were completely compatible with each other. Both were egotistical, conniving, and snobbish, finding faults in everyone but themselves. They both wanted rich mates and discovering that the other had a great fortune, the deal was sealed. Whether love was factored into the equation was an entirely different matter.

Having read enough, Mary closed the letter and sat in contemplation. "Mr. Quigley and Miss Phillips are to be married," she breathed aloud. "Quite a peculiar match, if I do say so."

"Mr. Quigley and Miss Phillips?" the nurse echoed. "Peculiar the match might be, but is it one made in heaven?" Mary shook her head.

"Possibly," she replied, rising to her feet. "But they need to get their acts together before they exchange vows, or their children will be drowned in their voracity."

Tapping the letter against her palm, Mary prepared to ascend the stairs, then turned to give Dolly the letter. When it touched Dolly's fingers, Mary intoned seriously, "Oh, and you did not allow the wax to dry enough after resealing the invitation." Looking up, the maid found

Mary waving her waxy fingers in the air before she departed for her room.

Later that day, Mary left her chamber to enter her father's study so as to read more of the letters. It always excited her when she opened the green box, feeling like it was the very first time each time she popped open the lid. She grabbed a handful of letters that she had not yet read, and sitting contentedly in her father's chair, her eyes scanned every line of the writing.

Jan. 4th, 1818
My Young Lieutenant,

I must admit, I was very much surprised at your arrival in London this past week. Mother and Father did not know what to expect since they considered my explanations of you 'over exaggerated'. As for me, I was a nervous wreck when you showed up, not especially in my finest hour. Of course you picked the one day I decided to explore my creative side and paint with pastels. But everything worked out for the best and my family adores you, though not as much as I do. You've confirmed my notions of British people, however: peculiar, yet endearing all the same. I only hope this pleasure could be shared again, but I ask that you inform me of your visits before you appear at my doorstep again. I do love surprises, but not when dressed like a total slob in the presence of an enchanting character. You said you'd find me beautiful whatever I looked like, but I'd like to point out that you're not a woman, therefore you lack in any understanding of the subject. Do write to me, my Young Lieutenant, as I look forward to your lines. I'd be fibbing if I said I wasn't praying for your injury to worsen so you can spend more time with me. It's selfish, yes, but you'd expect nothing less of your Pioneer.

Yours truly,
Rosemary Smith

8 January 1818
My dear Pioneer,

I delight in my attempts to mortify you, but as you wish, I will inform you in advance of future visits to London. As far as everything else is concerned, there's not especially anything exciting to report other than my support for America. I refuse to subject myself to change, since I had sworn my allegiance to England, but as we stubbornly refuse to disband from the land, I cannot help but feel somewhat foul for my actions. But I will be soon discharged of my services, I believe, because a certain little Pioneer has prayed for my injury to worsen. Much

*obliged, by the way. But I do look forward to seeing you
again, Rosemary. Your family is a delight and I crave for
stimulating conversation, ending in satirical rants. Be safe
and you can stop praying for my side to hurt; it aches me
enough now, thank you. I will write to you again as soon
as possible.*

Love always,
Your Young Lieutenant

Hour after hour, she would read these notes; there were
so many of them to go through. But she would stop herself
if she was ruffling through them too fast, because she
wanted to make them last as long as she possibly could.

After finishing one of her mother's letters, there was a
knock on the door and Dolly informed her that dinner was
served. Immediately, she packed away the letters into the
green box, gently placed it back into the drawer, and
locked it. Exiting the study, she met with the servants and
they all stood up, bowed, and then sat down after she had
done so. They waited for a few more of the servants to
arrive, then heard Dolly knock on a door. "Mr.
Rodchester," she called. "Barney? Supper's ready; do you
want to join us or do you want me to bring something up
for you?" She listened for an answer, but none came. One
of the younger servants, Aimee Landstrom, passed Dolly
and questioned if everything was alright. "I suppose so,"

the nurse replied uncertainly. "He usually rejoices at the mere mention of food. Must have been a long day in town."

"He does get sidetracked when he delivers anything to town," Aimee reminded. "He probably is exhausted from telling one of his sailor stories to the young mariners."

"Possibly," Dolly agreed, "but I'm going to check up on him anyway."

Reaching for the handle, Dolly pushed on it to go in, but the door was locked. Again, she knocked, calling to him even louder, but she still received no response. Concern began to well up inside her.

"Mr. Clark! Mr. Brackle!" she called down to the group. "Can you come and help me, please?" Straight away, two of the younger, more strapping servants ascended the stairs to assist Dolly. "I can't get the door open," she said to them once they arrived, "and he won't answer."

"Is he even in there?" Mr. Brackle inquired as Mr. Clark jiggled the handle. "He has locked himself out of his room before."

"Please," Dolly begged. "Put my mind at ease and open the blasted door."

Obediently, the men complied and walking to the halfway point of the hall, they both rammed the door, full force, with their bodies. The door was no match, as they knocked it off its hinges. Looking up, after rubbing their shoulders, they noticed the servant sleeping in his bed.

"There, you see?" Mr. Clark said to her, rising to his feet. "He was only sleeping."

"That, or he's especially drunk tonight," Mr. Brackle added.

But Dolly would not be satisfied until she heard directly from Mr. Rodchester himself. Coming up from behind him, she shook him to wake, but he still would not stir. She shook him further, rolling him on his back. Terror would not begin to describe Dolly's reaction as she screamed at the top of her lungs, nearly falling backwards at the sight of what lay before her. Mr. Brackle and Mr. Clark were shocked, too, fixing their eyes upon their boss lying on the bed. There, in the middle of the old servant's chest, a large knife stood straight up within a pool of blood. Curiosity from the outside soon trickled inside the room as all the servants, as well as Mary, felt the aching sensation of seeing one of their own brutally murdered.

Only one of them was composed enough to shout out orders to aid Mr. Rodchester. "Find Dr. Eastworthy!" Mr. Kent turned to Dolly. "Wadsworth," he continued, "go and get the police. Sarah, find the undertaker. Go! Quickly!"

As they were ordered, the servants disbanded, while the others wept at Mr. Rodchester's door. Mary's heart sank further than any of the others as she turned away from the body, unable to look at it any longer. She hoped that someone had an explanation and that the perpetrator would be found before any more souls were lost.

Chapter Fifteen

*T*he doctor was the first to arrive. He scurried out of his carriage and made his way up to Mr. Rodchester's room. He was pale, even sickly looking, for he sniffled and his eyes sagged. Pushing aside his physical condition, he rushed to Mr. Rodchester's room and entered.

He was upset, to be sure, as he set his medical bag down before examining the servant. Though his eyes were drained of both color and energy, they displayed compassion as he carefully checked for any signs of life, though in his heart he knew there was little chance of it.

In the street below, all kinds of questions were being raised in the neighbors' minds. They had heard Dolly's screams, and peered out their windows, some even coming outside so as to get a better look from the street. As they peered up, they could sometimes see the movements of Dr. Eastworthy through Mr. Rodchester's window. There was speculation as to what might have occurred; some wondered what might happen next. The people standing outside soon returned indoors, then continued to watch through their windows.

As for the doctor, he finished his examination within a few minutes, then shook his head in disappointment. "I'm sorry," he said with a sniffle. "But there's nothing I can do."

Those were the words the servants had dreaded to hear. They looked to one another for comfort but could find no peace as their eyes turned back to the doctor. Dolly disconsolately dropped her head to her chest, still containing her tears, and thanked Dr. Eastworthy for all his help.

As she spoke, there was another slam of a carriage door. A minute later, they heard voices from the floor below. "Right this way," Mr. Lou said, leading in two officers.

Looking over, they all saw Mr. Adams and Mr. Quinnley approaching. Mr. Adams was the older of the two, about Jonathan Wheaton's age, and Quinnley two years older than Mary. They were the only law enforcers in the area; though Denny's Grove was large, most of the cases involved simple domestic incidents.

As they walked into the room and saw Mr. Rodchester's massacred body, they shook their heads, and turned to the doctor for his report.

"What news do you have on the victim, Doc?" Mr. Adams was first to speak. Dr. Eastworthy coughed.

"He's dead," he replied, wiping his mouth, "if that's the answer you're looking for. He's been dead for hours." The men exchanged glances, while the doctor went into another coughing fit.

Approaching the body, the two men examined it themselves, observing the rum and whiskey bottles scattered near the side of the bloody bed. "Still quite the drinker," Mr. Quinnley remarked, pushing aside the bottles with his foot. "Does he drink himself to sleep?"

"Sometimes," Mr. Brackle admitted with a roll of the head. "In Scotland, his parents would give him a shot of whiskey to put him to sleep." Mr. Adams raised his eyebrows.

Continuing his inspection, he touched the knife, then Mr. Rodchester's clothes. He could smell the alcohol amongst the other smells. "He was drinking when he died," Mr. Adams indicated. Turning to the doctor, he asked, "Could you smell that, too?"

"I can't smell anything," the doctor confessed, sneezing into his handkerchief. "But I'll take your word for it."

"It's not uncommon for Mr. Rodchester to return home drunk," Mr. Clark sadly spoke. "He goes to town with entertaining tales of both land and sea. Oftentimes, his listeners buy him a drink as he tells his stories. He must have had one especially interested listener."

"Or an especially irked one," Quinnley added, jotting down the servant's comments in his notebook. "Does anyone know who Mr. Rodchester had been in contact with the night before?" the older officer broke in. There was a momentary pause.

"Countless people," Dolly spoke, breaking her long silence since their arrival. "As for who he was with last night, you would have to ask at the various taverns. All of the owners know him."

Standing in quiet deliberation, interrupted only by Dr. Eastworthy's sniffles, the officers took another look around the room. They saw an overturned stool by the desk, but nothing else was out of the ordinary. Books were distributed all over the room as they normally were, and maps of the sea took up most of the right hand side of the servant's writing space. But as they were trying to deduce the means of entry, Mary broke through the group of curious servants. She avoided looking at the bloody corpse, and took courage as she spoke to Mr. Adams.

"I saw Mr. Rodchester last night," she timidly offered. The officers turned towards her, exchanging a quick glance with each other.

"You did?" the younger officer asked in a surprised tone. Mr. Adams rested a hand on his partner's arm to quiet him.

Taking a step towards Mary, he asked her in a very solemn tone, "Why were you in town?"

Mary sighed, still striving to keep her eyes from wandering towards Mr. Rodchester. She stood tongue-tied, feeling the body watch her as she stood there. The elder official, seeing her discomfort, suggested, "Why don't we go outside?"

Gratefully, Mary nodded, tightly closing her lids as she exited. She stood before the great window at the very top of the steps while the two men listened intently to her story. "I was just coming from Harlow's Restaurant after a meeting with Isabella Cantwell," Mary said in a shaky tone, "when Mr. Rodchester stopped me to ask what I was doing. He then proceeded to spew out some story about the undertaker and his son before I promised him I'd be careful when I returned home. I left him then, turning around once to make sure he wasn't too upset because I did not believe his tale, and saw three gentlemen speaking with him."

"Could you see who they were?" Quinnley inquired. Mary nodded.

"I think so," she said, fiddling with her fingers. "I believe I saw Mr. Winkleman, Mr. Fackleman, and Mr. Rolland listening to his tales." The younger officer furrowed his brow and scribbled down Mary's words.

"And he was completely sober when you spoke with him?" he asked and Mary nodded again.

They continued to question her for about ten minutes more. At first, the questions were general, as they inquired about what she had seen and heard. But then the queries became more personal, as they questioned her relationship with Mr. Rodchester. She tried to recall every detail, then run it over in her mind. But pretty soon she doubted what she had remembered. The officers weren't of much help to her nerves, either. After they had shot one question at her and waited for an answer, another came her way. Suspicious glances, muffled 'hmms', and daunting glares were just a few of the things they did to discomfit her. Instead of helping her, it felt like they were suspecting her.

Soon, they dismissed her, first thanking her for her cooperation. Before they could discuss the case themselves, however, Dr. Eastworthy went into another coughing fit, completely disrupting their train of thought. He apologized with a sniffle, wiping his nose. Mr. Adams assured him that there was nothing further for him to be concerned about. "Quinnley and I will handle this from here."

"You should get some rest," Dolly broke in. "Take care of that cold before it takes care of you."

Nodding, the doctor buried his face in his handkerchief and exited, first bowing towards Mary before descending the stairs. "My deepest condolences, Miss Wheaton," the doctor called over to her. "If there's anything you need, don't hesitate to ask."

Dolly led him out, while the officers returned to the scene of the crime, going over the list of witnesses that they would need to question. There were the three men that Mary had seen talking with Mr. Rodchester, the bartenders, as well as other miscellaneous souls whose names might crop up as a result of their upcoming interviews.

As they were discussing their approach to the case, the servants stirred, having heard a disturbance outside. They peered out the great window, trying to determine the source of the noise. In the distance, they could hear the neighing of horses and the rush of hooves, followed by loud strikes of a whip and the driver's shouts. The servants strained to peer through the darkness, observing the shadows of some approaching object. "Death be here," Mr. Kent breathed, as everyone looked out. "And he comes with his son."

Suddenly, they heard a door slam, and all turned towards the main entrance. It wasn't long before Mrs. Lou rushed in with a man dressed all in black, behind her. She quickly shut the door behind the man, who turned out to be Nicholas Black, and directed him to the dead servant's room. "He's just up the stairs and to the right," she pointed.

He paused a moment, took off his bowler hat and bowed, making his way up the stairs. Mary and the servants watched as he scaled the steps. He passed by the servants without any acknowledgement, their eyes closely following him. Mary watched him discreetly, letting her eyes travel towards his until they met. She locked gazes with him and found herself shuddering when he bowed to her.

As he entered Mr. Rodchester's room, all conversation ceased and all eyes were on him. Nicholas glanced over towards Mr. Rodchester's body, before looking away. He inspected the room before turning his attention to Mr. Adams and Mr. Quinnley. "Mr. Black," Mr. Adams guardedly greeted. "So good of you to join us."

The undertaker nodded at him but said nothing as he approached Mr. Rodchester's body. He placed on surgical gloves before examining the corpse.

Feeling a chill come over them, the servants -- save Dolly, Mr. Kent, and Mr. and Mrs. Lou -- disbanded, choosing to return to their chambers rather than hover so close to Nicholas. Mary, nonetheless, kept her position by the door, watching with curiosity as the undertaker carefully inspected the body.

He was cautious, making sure he didn't disturb the environment as he moved around. When he was done, he raised his head, stuffed his gloves into his pocket and declared, "You can remove the knife."

A bit hesitantly, Mr. Quinnley stepped forward and grabbed the knife-handle, pulling at it, though there was little sign of movement on the weapon's part. He tried again and again, but it would not budge. Mr. Adams assisted him, but the two men were still no match.

As the two officers continued their efforts with the knife, Mr. Kent stepped forward to ask Nicholas, "Your thoughts appear to be different from theirs. What do *you* think about this?"

Nicholas turned to him, looking away from the body for a moment, and replied simply, "I'm not aware of Mr. Adam's and Mr. Quinnley's thoughts."

Then moving towards the body, Nicholas grasped the knife and pulled it out with one swift motion, handing it to Mr. Adams before continuing his conversation with the servant. "But I suppose I can guess at their thoughts," he said. "They assumed he was drunk and hence easily overpowered."

"How did you do that?!" the shocked young officer asked, as he examined the knife. The other two ignored him.

"That's about right," Mr. Kent replied. "They suppose the perpetrator deliberately got him drunk."

"Oh," Nicholas said with a hint of sarcasm, "so they think *one* man did this?" The servant stared at him in disbelief.

"Do you suppose more than one was involved?" he questioned. Nicholas shrugged but didn't reply.

The officers soon excused themselves, descended the stairs, and continued a heated discussion of the case in the foyer. Mary sat down on the sill of the great window, overcome by sorrow. She felt an ache far deeper than any she had ever experienced before. Seeing death first hand, especially a murder, caused a sting that only added to the pain she had felt since her father's passing. Her mind was lost in deep thought and her eyes were unfocussed. She had thought that if she stayed in Denny's Grove things would change for the better.

Tears were rolling down her face when Nicholas approached from behind her. She flinched, seeing his reflection in the window, and turned to face him. Far from composed, she found herself speaking to him. "Mr. Black," she said tearfully, "you frightened me."

His solemn stare turned to one of compassion. Taking a seat next to her, he withdrew a handkerchief from his jacket and offered it to her. Gratefully she took it and apologized for her state. "Don't apologize," Nicholas replied quickly. "You have every right to be upset."

"Yes," Mary agreed, wiping her eyes, "but people usually wait until no one else is in the room before they completely break down."

Nicholas did not remove his gaze as he replied, "Some unwritten rule I'm unaware of?" She smiled slightly, then lapsed into silence. "I want you to take him from here," she said finally, wiping away the last of her tears. "It just hurts too much to see him in this house." Nicholas nodded.

"I understand," he said, and was going to leave when she called back to him.

"And Mr. Black," she said, "if it's possible, can we please have the funeral within the week?" The undertaker lowered his eyes and bowed to her. He walked over to the hearse, then returned to the house with a stretcher. This time, he was accompanied by a tall man in black who kept his face concealed. The pair took the body of Mr. Rodchester away and loaded him up in the hearse.

Before Nicholas climbed up into the driver's seat, he overheard the two officers' conversation. "Mr. Rolland was a witness in Mr. Parker's murder, and now he was one of the last to see Rodchester alive," Mr. Adams said. "That seems a bit fishy, doesn't it?"

"But how could he have possibly done it?" Mr. Quinnley asked. "Did he climb up to the servant's room, because someone would have seen him? I think it was an inside job, willful entry."

"Are you suggesting…"

"Miss Wheaton, yes," Mr. Quinnley interrupted. "Think about it: the girl knew both Mr. Parker and Mr. Rodchester. Many of the servants spoke of Miss Wheaton's and Mr. Rodchester's close friendship."

"Oh, but Mary is a good girl, she would never…"

Mr. Adams trailed off into thought, now considering Mary as a possible suspect in the crime. He was still with his thoughts when he was interrupted by a voice from behind. "That's all fine," the voice said, "but who would the second perpetrator be?"

Turning, the two men found Nicholas behind them, his hands casually behind his back, looking at them with a raised eyebrow. Mr. Adams glared at him. "What do you mean 'second perpetrator'?" he asked, somewhat annoyed. Nicholas shrugged his shoulders, looking up at the night sky.

"There are two individuals who took part in the crime," he said, still gazing at the stars. The officers exchanged glances.

"How do you know that?" Quinnley spoke up. The undertaker explained himself.

"There was a red mark on his neck," he said simply. "One strangled him, while the other stabbed."

"One person still could have done it," Mr. Adams countered. "He could have strangled him first, and then stabbed him. Or just stabbed him. Who says he couldn't have gotten that mark from elsewhere?"

"I estimate Mr. Rodchester weighed around 270 pounds," Nicholas said, now facing them. "Most of his weight is in muscle. You're saying that he wouldn't have fought off his attacker? And you suggest that Miss Wheaton was this attacker?"

"It had to be someone whom Rodchester would have invited into his quarters," Mr. Adams retorted defensively. "Don't rule out Miss Wheaton. She could have easily drugged him or paid off the servants, for that matter. Besides, it's *our* job to discover the means by which the man died, not *yours*."

Thinking they had silenced him, the two officers climbed onto their carriage without another word. But before

Quinnley could order the horses on, Nicholas calmly called out, "I wouldn't think you to be the one to discredit the family that saved your life, Mr. Adams. But then again, I'm just an undertaker. What do *I* know?"

Bowing to the men, Nicholas turned away and climbed into the driver's seat of the hearse. Mr. Adams watched as the horses disappeared in the mist, then instructed Quinnley to take off. It was nearly one in the morning when they finally departed.

Chapter Sixteen

*T*he next day started uneventfully. The servants went about their duties, without breathing as much as a 'hello' to one another, just striving to finish what they had started. They hoped, perhaps, that this day might bring more comforting tidings.

Meanwhile, Mary sat in her father's study with the drawer of letters. She opened the box to read away her sorrow, but couldn't find it in herself to open the next letter in the series. So, she sat and stared into emptiness, clinging to the key given her by Mr. Parker.

At that point, she was at a loss as to what to do. Her father was gone, and her childhood friend murdered. She could approach Dolly or Morgan with her troubles, but their consolation could only extend so far.

For the next couple of days, Wheaton Manor was shrouded in silence. There was no sign of activity, other than the outdoor workers. A few curious souls would glance at the home as they strolled by, only to turn their attention back to the task at hand, thoughts of Wheaton Manor haunting them for the remainder of the day.

Gossip was bound to circulate, what with the doctor, the police, and the undertaker having been seen visiting the residence. Some speculated that Miss Wheaton had committed suicide, while others thought that one of the servants -- Rodchester perhaps -- had killed her. Although witnesses questioned the next day by Mr. Adams and Mr. Quinnley cleared up these rumors, still they continued to spread.

What the real story was, no one really knew, but each story that passed by Morgan's ear concerned her. The day after Rodchester's murder, she called upon the Wheaton home, only to be turned down. She tried again and again, trying to pry information from the servants about what had happened, but without success. Finally, after the fifth day of hearing nothing, Morgan had had enough and journeyed to the home to find out for herself.

When she arrived, the gates were closed. She thought of scaling them, but there were jagged edges at the top. She then studied the grounds to see if the servants had filled the hole that she, Mary, and Timothy had dug as children in order to sneak into the Manor whenever Mary's father had locked the gates. The bush that camouflaged the hole was still there, and she pushed aside the flowers and branches to discover the opening.

But before she took her chances with the dirt, she saw Dolly emerge from the home with a basket of linens. Morgan tried to get her attention by waving her arms as she ran along the fence, frantically calling, "Dolly! Dolly! Over here!"

Turning, Dolly saw Morgan waving through the fence. The servant lowered her basket, strolled over to the fence warily, and keeping her distance from the bars, asked her, "What are you doing here, Miss Greenwood?"

Morgan gripped the metallic bars and replied, "I've been trying to call upon Mary for the past five days! All sorts of rumors are going around town and they're so distorted that they're concerning me. The only report that seems to remain consistent is that there has been a murder. Is everyone alright? Is Mary okay?"

Dolly did not respond. She thought about what to say, looking around to see if anyone else was listening. Then, moving closer to the fence, she whispered, "You didn't hear it from me, but yes, one of our servants was murdered. Miss Mary is just fine; and now you may rest easy."

Dolly moved to leave, but Morgan reached through the bars and grabbed her wrist, forbidding her to leave before she gave her the answers she wanted. "You do realize that Mary is my best friend, Dolly, right?" Morgan said with blazing eyes. "If you don't let me in to speak with her, I'll find some other means, believe me."

"But Miss Wheaton desires to see no one," the servant argued, anxiously surveying the grounds. "What am I to say to her when you appear at her doorway by means of the back gate?" Morgan instantly released the servant, taking the hint.

"Thank you," she whispered gratefully. Running towards the back of the home, she entered the gate and made her way to the house.

She scampered up the stairs to Mary's room, feeling she'd find her there, but the room was empty. Morgan then ran across the hall to Mr. Rodchester's room and opened it. Benny was there, but no Mary.

"Could she have slipped out and gone to the cemetery?" she wondered. Then a fresh thought came to mind. "Mr. Wheaton's study!"

Closing Mr. Rodchester's room, Morgan dashed down the stairs and into the study to find Mary on the floor by the drawer with the letters. Her eyes were streaming with tears as she turned towards Morgan, very much surprised to see her.

But Morgan said nothing as she fell to her knees and embraced her friend, feeling the tremors of Mary's body through the rush of tears and sadness. Peace finally came to Mary as she hugged her friend, clinging tightly to her as the tears poured. Nothing needed to be said; their closeness was enough.

While Morgan was consoling Mary, Mr. Quinnley appeared at the front door, anxiously fidgeting with his hat. "I'll go fetch her for you, Mr. Quinnley," Dolly said, and she left him in the foyer while she sought out Mary.

She found her still in the study, with Morgan by her side, and told Mary that Mr. Quinnley had arrived to update her concerning the case. Mary quickly wiped her face, adjusted her hair and clothes so as to be presentable, and greeted the officer with a curtsy.

He appeared sad as he looked at her. Seeing that her eyes were red and puffy from sobbing, he bowed to her, and inquired, "How do you fare, Miss Wheaton?" Mary swallowed and struggled for a smile.

"I've been better," she admitted in a cheerless tone. Mr. Quinnley frowned.

"Forgive me," he continued after a brief pause, "but I come alone, since Mr. Adams had some business to attend to. He sends his apologies."

"That's alright," Mary responded. "Any news?"

Hesitantly, the officer shook his head and related to her the progress that he and his partner had made to date. "We spoke with the various tavern owners in town," he said wiping a hand behind his neck, "and found that Mr. Rodchester was last seen at Avery's before returning home. Sylvester was bartending that night, but only gave him two beers. No one was with him. We also spoke with Misters Fackleman, Winkleman, and Rolland, whom you've said you saw speaking with him last. From what they've said, Mr. Rodchester had been telling them a story of a storm. They told me what it was, but it was nothing that would stir any emotions. What it comes down to, though, is: We have no suspects, Miss."

Mary dropped her head in disappointment, but she thanked Quinnley for his, as well as Mr. Adams', hard work. He was clearly upset as he put his hat back on. "I'm sorry," he said to her. "We'll keep our ears peeled, but as of now, there's nothing more we can do. Good day, Miss."

Tipping his hat to her, Mr. Quinnley exited and Dolly closed the door behind him, peering over to Mary in distress. She carefully watched Mary as she stood, eyes fixed upon nothingness. She rested a hand on her shoulder, breaking her out of her trance. "Come now," she said to Mary. "Let's get you ready for lunch." Turning to Morgan, she asked, "Will you be joining us?" Morgan shook her head.

"No," she replied. "I think it's best if I leave."

Following Mr. Quinnley's steps outside, Morgan left Dolly and Mary in the foyer. They stood there for a while too, since Mary would not move, but eventually, the nurse pushed her up the steps and into her room where she got her dressed. Tomorrow would be Mr. Rodchester's funeral.

Chapter Seventeen

*T*he funeral was not as difficult as Mary had imagined. Yes, she saw Mr. Rodchester's body for the first time since the murder, but she was calm, having already spent her tears earlier that day.

"He looks so much at peace," Dolly remarked to Mary as they neared the coffin. They studied him, seeing how his face now appeared twenty years younger. They rested a hand on his, saying a little prayer over him. Mary kissed his head; Dolly remained where she was, absorbed in her prayer, and heavily exhaled, saying some of her words aloud so that Mary could hear. "You were more than a good man," she said to him with eyes still closed, "you were family. May the good Lord watch over you and keep you safe. But I swear, if you jump out of this coffin and scare the living tart out of me, I will grab one of these candles and set you afire. Amen."

She then opened her eyes and walked with Mary to their pew. "Heartfelt prayer, Dolly," she observed. "I think you just tempted him.

When everyone had had their time with Mr. Rodchester, the priest proceeded with the eulogy. He had no personal connection to the deceased servant, but he could clearly see that the man was well loved by many.

He said some lovely prayers and gave Mr. Rodchester a blessing, then inquired whether anyone had any words they would like to say about him. Quickly, one of Rodchester's drinking buddies volunteered, and making his way through the people in his pew, waddled up to the podium.

He was a scruffy-looking, six-foot tall man with flaming red hair, who went by the name of Seamore McCarrier. He had sailed the seas with Rodchester, encouraging the servant's stories with glasses of rum and old Scottish tunes. Though also known as a town drunk, he was not as crazy as the recently-deceased.

As he situated himself at the stand, he laid his arms upon it and spoke in a manner that was more intelligible than Mr. Rodchester's ever was. "Frien's, family, and impertinent people," he started out. "I have to tell ye aboot the first time I met my good frien' Rodchester. Aye! Barney was a young scallywag, he was, whe' he first stepped on the *Alma May*. The cap'n nearly threw his ars seaport whe' Barney nailed doon his pegged leg! Ye remember tha', Hindley?!"

"Good show, Old Bean!" a man shouted from the crowd.

Mr. McCarrier smiled and went on, "Aye! Aye! It was clear from the begi'ing tha' Rodchester be no land lubber. He was born fer the seas and she meant to be his bride. I wood remember how he wood scare the newer kin by prete'ing to be brutally stabbed! Oh, what a braw fellow! May Jock Tamson keep him! Amen."

He stepped down, and the congregation stared at him with puzzled looks on their faces. Mary, however, snickered under her breath and watched as the priest hesitantly stepped back into position at the podium.

"Thank you, Mr. McCarrier, for that interesting deliverance," he said with a bob of his eyebrows. Turning to the rest of the crowd, he inquired, "Would anyone else like to say anything about Barney Rodchester?"

Indeed, five more individuals came forward with something to say about the servant. Most of them weren't as eccentric as Seamore, though they did have entertaining tales to narrate. Afterwards, the priest gave Rodchester the final blessing before everyone exited the church to reconvene at the cemetery.

Dolly stood by Mary the whole time as they went out, keeping a close eye on her mistress in case she suddenly broke down, but Mary was very much composed as they neared the burial ground. Her mind seemed to be at ease and her heart serene when she stood before the hole. She and the servants kept close to the coffin as it was lowered into its place. Seamore and a few of the other retired

sailors played the bagpipes for their friend, while the elder
Mr. Black and his son began to throw soil over the now-
lowered coffin.

The ceremony was soon over, and the people began to
leave. A few paused to offer their sympathies to Mary.
Morgan was the first to do so, as she embraced her. Mary
thanked her for attending and Morgan smiled, responding,
"Of course. I'll miss him interrupting our card games with
his lunatic rants. Those were some of my favorite times."
Mary agreed and Morgan hugged her again, followed in
turn by her older brother and his wife.

"I'm so sorry for your loss, Miss Mary," Mr. Winkleman
said after they had gone. "Rodchester's stories were most
entertaining." He bowed and she nodded, turning to the
next person in line, who happened to be Jane Phillips.

"Oh Mary!" she cried, dramatically throwing her arms
around her. "How horrible you must feel! *I* can never
imagine the excruciating pain you must be experiencing
right now. I would ache with sadness and blame myself for
such a terrible thing to occur in my very own home! What
sorrow! What anguish!"

She released Mary who stared at her for a moment
before replying, "Thank you, Miss Phillips; you always
know what to say."

"My pleasure," she responded, putting a hand to her
shoulder. She then pulled out her handkerchief, brushed

away imaginary tears, then moved on as Eliza Orchid approached.

"Oh, you poor dear!" Eliza cried to the skies, also hugging her. "Bugaloo was such a dear."

"Barney," Mary corrected. Eliza was lost in her own words to even hear.

"Yes," she went on, "Barnaby will be truly missed."

When Eliza had departed, Mary was left alone with Dolly. Mary gratefully turned to her, sighing with relief that it had not been too agonizing of a burial. "How do you feel, dear?" Dolly guardedly asked her.

Mary tilted her head as she looked up towards the sky, responding, "Better. I think the most painful experience just left with Miss Orchid."

The servant handed Mary her hat and gloves, and looked one last time towards the gravesite before she said to her mistress, "Shall we go?"

"I suppose so," Mary calmly responded. "There's not much to do now but to move on with life. He would want it that way; I know it. But I'd like to stop in the church and say a little prayer before I go. I'll only be a moment."

Handing her things to Dolly, Mary made her way back to the little church on the grounds and peeked in before entering. It was dead silent when she moved down the aisle. All the candles had been burnt out, except for the two on the altar, and the quiet interior aided her own tranquility.

As she turned her head to the left, she suddenly stopped; Nicholas Black was kneeling in the very front pew, deep in prayer. One of his hands completely covered his face while the other dangled, still clasping his hat. She was hesitant to move forward, so she simply swallowed any fear and sat down on a bench nearest her to say a few prayers.

Her head lowered and her eyes closed as she thought about Rodchester. She smiled and thanked God for her time with him, recounting her stories to Him as if He had not already heard them before. She also talked with Rodchester, telling him that things would most certainly never be the same without him, but that she would do her best to cope and keep a watchful eye on the staff at the Manor.

Saying her last good-bye, she exited the pew, looked to the left and noticed that Nicholas was no longer there. She moved towards the door, her eyes still fixed on the altar. Finally turning, she was startled to find Nicholas standing in front of her. He said nothing, simply bowed to her and held open the door so she could leave. She thanked him, quickly made her way back to her carriage, and dared not look back for fear of seeing him watching her.

Life at Wheaton Manor soon returned to something approaching normal. Complete normalcy would not come until much later; in the meantime, everyone took life a day at a time.

Chapter Eighteen

*T*alk of the funeral ceased as quickly as it had come up, and now the residents of Denny's Grove turned their attention to the upcoming ball at Douglas Rolland's home. Of all the citizens, he invariably threw the most extravagant parties. He took great pride in it and would go out of his way to outdo anyone who dared to challenge him.

Mr. Rolland was very handsome: tall, well-built, and lean. He had dark brown hair, green eyes, and a mustache that was always carefully groomed. But he wasn't the most agreeable type of person. He considered himself the ideal man of the century, and was known to share this opinion with his friends and acquaintances.

But people attended his balls regardless, always intrigued by the splendor he felt obliged to provide them. Once past his greeting at the door, his guests reckoned he could easily be avoided. After all, he was just one person among the hundreds present.

"Are you going to Mr. Rolland's ball, Mary?" Morgan asked her as they walked to the Songbird Village.

"It's a bit too soon to return to revelry," Mary responded. "I think I might stay home that night." Morgan frowned.

"I understand your feelings," replied Morgan, "but it will get your mind off of what has happened."

"I highly doubt that!" Mary cried. "It'll only make me more anxious anyway. You should go without me."

Mary walked on in silence, now approaching the St. Xavier's Cemetery. She groaned, wanting so badly for Rodchester to be with her now. Morgan felt her friend's sadness, too, as she watched her stare at the cemetery plots. But tearing her gaze away from the grounds, Mary determinedly walked on.

"You need some cheering up, dear," Morgan declared, breaking the silence. "Besides, Mr. Rolland's ball is still two weeks away; you might change your mind by then."

Mary raised her head, but didn't reply. Perhaps Morgan had a point. There was no use keeping herself locked up in her house when life was just waiting for her around the next corner. She needed some joy in her life, after all, and the thought that Morgan would be there with her, comforted her tremendously.

Raising her eyes to the skies, Mary took in a deep breath and replied, "Oh, perhaps you're right, Morgan. I really haven't done much to get over my father's passing, and now that Rodchester's gone, I fear I might repeat the whole process over again. It's no good if I seclude myself from society."

They soon arrived at the Songbird Village, where Mary and Morgan parted company, the former returning home to Denny's Grove, savoring every step she took along the way.

The breeze was light and the air tranquil as she slowly made her way back. Only a few clouds floated through the skies, and the chirping of the birds greeted her as she passed by. All thoughts were lost in the beauty, and all cares drifted with the winds. She looked towards the moors, which stretched to her left, and found herself skipping on her way towards them.

When her feet touched the gentle grasses, she removed her shoes and ran as fast as she could. She danced and twirled on the grass, throwing her hands into the air in delight. Suddenly coming upon a cave, she looked in, curious to see what lay inside, but found nothing but rocks. One spot, however, in the middle of the cave, grabbed her attention. Light entering through the roof fell upon a small plot of ground where flowers and shamrocks grew. She approached it, noting how peculiar it was to find such vegetation in this secluded spot. Suddenly, with a loud rumble of thunder from above, her light source vanished and she was left in complete darkness as a random summer storm raced through the area. Thunder cracked through the skies like a whip, and water pelted the ground; but she felt safe in the cavern.

Mary sat on the ground while she watched and waited, delighting in the storm's power and its intriguing light show. Raising herself, she could see shepherds in the distance herding their sheep to escape the cascading water bombarding them from above. And she could not help but look, as nature persisted to please her, but it wasn't long before water was trickling its way through the roof of the cave and dripping on top of her head. She moved away from all the cracks and crevices in the ceilings, and edged her way closer to the cave entrance. After a few minutes wait, the sun broke out between the clouds, and the birds resumed their chirping.

Rising to her feet, Mary placed her shoes on and emerged from the cave. She gazed at the grassy moors as the sunlight glistened through the little water droplets. Taking the path to her village, she wrung the water out of her dress and dried off by the time she reached the cemetery.

In the distance, she saw an approaching figure, with a bare chest and a shovel over his shoulder. For a moment, she thought it was Mr. Clark or Mr. Brackle, since the man appeared strong. Taking a closer look, however, she saw that he was younger and shorter than either of them.

When he was close enough, Mary could see that it was Nicholas Black. He must have been caught in the rainstorm because he looked drenched from head to toe. He was courteous as always, halting to bow to her before he continued on his way.

"Work in the graveyard again, Mr. Black?" Mary said as he passed her.

He stopped, turned toward her, and merely replied, "Yes, Miss." Mary shifted her weight. "You know, it's not always good to constantly immerse yourself in cheerless settings," she said. "I do understand your line of work, but do you ever come into town for any sort of leisurely activity?"

"I find being in town no different than spending my time in the graveyard," Nicholas replied. Mary tilted her head.

"Oh?" she replied. "How so?"

"All conversation is dead to me," he answered. Mary chuckled uncomfortably. His expression, though, was unchanged.

Clearing her throat to relieve the awkwardness, she said to him, "Very well then; have it your way. But there is one thing the town can offer that the cemetery cannot: lively spirits."

She smiled and curtsied, then continued on her way back to Wheaton Manor. Nicholas watched her until she was out of his sight, then moved towards the graveyard. Entering the stable, he set aside his shovel, and went directly to work.

Chapter Nineteen

*T*he day arrived that almost everyone had been waiting for. Women did their last minute shopping in the ribbon stores, while the men kept a low profile until they were dragged off to partake of the festivities in Scisserioux.

Meanwhile at Wheaton Manor, Mary and Morgan were being readied by Dolly and Mrs. Lou. Dolly curled Mary's hair, while Mrs. Lou braided and arranged pretty accessories in Morgan's. The girls were delighted to have a change of scenery and wondered what Douglas had to offer to his public this time.

"He must have had exquisite treats brought in from all around the world," Morgan conjectured. "Such a waste, when Denny's Grove and Rothbury have such lovely cuisines."

"Money, I'm guessing, is no object to him," Mary commented. "That seems to be the story of most well-to-do gentlemen these days."

"Perhaps they are attempts at flattery," Morgan teased, but Mary waved it off.

"Oh, you are cheeky!" she replied. "I have not been bothered by gentlemen regarding my father's money for nearly a month now, and I'm greatly enjoying it. It's all they think about these days: money and women. Either the wealth has to be boundless, or the woman's beauty unimaginable, in order to stir interest. Even if a woman does display considerable beauty, the man is more likely to go after a less-handsome one if she represents greater wealth."

Finishing the last of their hair, the servants left the girls to their final preparations in Mary's chamber. Dolly wished them a good time while Mrs. Lou gathered the room's linens and started the laundry.

"Maybe we'll find some answers today," Morgan said as she shut the door to Mary's room. Her friend stared at her in puzzlement, wondering what she could mean.

"What do you mean?" she asked, disappearing into her closet. Morgan continued, louder, so Mary could hear.

"I mean to say that there will be drinking at the ball," she replied. "Everyone's character is revealed then. We can find out anything we want by exploiting their drunkenness."

"The things we wish to find out most will be contained within the sober individuals, though," Mary pointed out.

"Remember, they are most on their guard when people like you come along."

Emerging from her closet, Mary twirled around in a simple white gown, seeking Morgan's approval. "Why don't you wear the one with the gold lace?" Morgan suggested. "It's rather pretty."

"I almost forgot about that one," Mary replied, going back into her closet. She removed the white dress while Morgan maintained the conversation.

"I daresay we'll see some revelation of character," she said with a toss of the head. "Some people cannot keep quiet if their lives depended on it."

"Do you delight in other people's mortifications?" Mary asked, peeking out.

Morgan shrugged her shoulders. "I empathize with those individuals who trustingly share a secret, but those who haven't the common decency to refrain from drunkenness only bring shame upon themselves. There will, indeed, be much to talk about!"

"Aha!" Mary suddenly broke in. She apparently frightened Morgan because the latter jumped, not expecting her friend to pop out of the closet just then.

With her dressing completed, Mary sat on the bed with her friend and smiled. "I have finally caught you!" she delightfully cried out. Morgan tilted her head.

"Caught me in what?" she asked.

"I finally caught you doing the most unspeakable thing: gossip." Morgan laughed off the comment.

"Oh," she said. "You know that's not what I meant."

"Not especially," Mary smiled. "From what I'm gathering, you want others to fall for your own amusement, so that you may then speak of them later -- gossip."

"I didn't mean it that way..."

"Gossip!"

"Am I the cheeky one? Well, it doesn't matter. Let's just drop the entire conversation before I further expose myself. Nice try, Miss Mary Wheaton."

Smiling, the two made some last minute adjustments to ready themselves, minutes before the ball began. The carriage had been prepared and was waiting for them the moment they stepped out, and with Mr. Kent as their driver, they were on their way to Mr. Rolland's party.

There were countless people who had arrived before the carriage pulled up to the mansion. They were all piling into the house, being greeted by Douglas at the front door, and beginning to dance and talk to their hearts' content.

Mary and Morgan were amazed by the exquisite beauty of the Rolland Mansion. It was now clear why everyone put up with Douglas' ways.

Looking up, the girls could see the beautiful architecture of the building. Vines and flowers were growing along its sides, and the surrounding acres were magnificently manicured. There were fountains in front of the house and in the back, with golden statues above and around them. It was like being in a palace, simply astounding!

As the girls basked in the home's beauty, the carriage came to a stop and Mr. Kent assisted them out. "Have a wonderful time," he said to them with a jolly smile. "But not too good of a time!"

"We will, gov'ner," Mary replied. She embraced him, and he kissed her on the head, bidding the two adieu.

Mr. Kent ordered his horses on. The girls exhaled in anticipation and reached for each other's hands. "Here we go," Morgan said to her friend. "This place is going to be heart-stopping indeed."

The two entered and were immediately spellbound. They were greeted by a fountain which towered high over their heads and a series of sculptures and paintings, boasting their glorious splendor. The marble floors seemed to stretch for miles, and every room they passed had ceilings which reached incredible heights. First timers gazed in awe at the architectural brilliance.

As they were marveling at the loveliness of the mansion, the girls were greeted by the host himself, Douglas Rolland. He was just as handsome as everyone had described; which put hopes in the hearts of all the young ladies present that reports concerning his ill-behavior were untrue.

He bowed to Mary and Morgan, and kissed their gloved hands, saying, "Miss Greenwood! Miss Wheaton! I am delighted to have you in my company. I hope you will enjoy yourselves."

"Thank you for your invitation, sir," Mary replied. "Your home is very beautiful."

"Exquisite, to say the least," Morgan broke in. Gratefully, Douglas bowed, and the women went on their way, continuing the exploration of the home, overwhelmed by its splendor.

Everything about Douglas' mansion pleased them: the food, drink, music and atmosphere. There were gentlemen everywhere, some appearing to be from out of town, as well as some from the village.

"Look," Morgan pointed, "there's Miss Phillips and Mr. Quigley. And over there, Dr. Eastworthy, Mr. Adams, Mr. Quinnley, Mrs. Parker, and Mrs. Reynolds. The whole town must be here!"

"And they very well could be," Mary responded, still in shock by the vastness of the estate. "I wonder if this was once part of the Buckingham home."

They had more than enough rooms to explore, but time may have been the only factor against them. They toured Scisserioux one room at a time, gazing at the people they passed along the way; watching gentlemen courting ladies, while the ladies giggled, shyly hiding behind their fans. Every now and then, they could hear the foot-taps of dancers in the adjoining area and the wail of violins as the players strung their chords. They lost themselves in the grandeur, and were caught unawares when Ian Hearn approached. He was quick to offer his greetings.

"Miss Greenwood, Miss Wheaton," he said with a disturbing grin. "It is a delight to see you both here." Turning to Mary, he added, "Pardon me, Miss Wheaton, but may I have the honor of dancing with you?"

Mary knew to expect this and threw a worried glance towards Morgan, who was trying to contain her laughter. She consented and went off with Mr. Hearn into the next room. She felt that the rest of the night was going to be filled with money-seeking bachelors as she stood across from her partner. It was not exactly the way she wished to spend her evening.

Before the song had scarcely begun, Ian made Mary feel especially uncomfortable. "I find you very ravishing tonight, Miss Wheaton," he said to her in an eerie tone. He swung around her, trying to be inconspicuous as he sniffed at her curls, then murmured to her, "Just as always."

Mary barely spoke a word to him as they danced. She would smile, or laugh uncomfortably whenever he talked to her, but she was wary as she watched for his hands, hoping that a pair of scissors wouldn't suddenly appear. She prepared herself for that possibility, but luckily for her, he did not snip off any of her hair that night.

It wasn't long before the dance ended and the two parted ways. Mary returned to find Morgan still seated on the sofa, the latter eager to hear how Mary had spent her time with Ian. "Not terrible," Mary admitted, pushing her hair out of her eyes. "His words were outlandish as always, but not terrible." Morgan stopped for a moment.

"Where are your gloves?" she asked, noticing Mary's bare hands. Looking down, Mary saw that the gloves were indeed missing. She knew she had them before the dance, because that was how she had planned to avoid touching Ian.

But considering whom she had been with, she said, "He must have taken them mid-dance when we were moving around in that circle." Morgan chuckled.

"He took your gloves?" she laughed. "How very strange!"

"I'm just relieved that he took those, instead of my hair," Mary declared and they strolled into another room. There, Morgan was asked to dance by a red coat, and she turned to Mary in worry, wondering if she should go or not. "Go, Morgan," Mary said. "I can very well take care of myself."

Exchanging a parting glance with her, Morgan went off, leaving Mary vulnerable to any gentlemen. Apparently, they had been waiting for Morgan to depart, for the moment Mary was alone, Mr. Inglis, Mr. MacDougal, Mr. Aaron, and Mr. Smith asked if they might have the next dance with her. Mary could not refuse them, though she wished she had; so she danced with all of them in turn. And each of them, in his own way, tried his hand at flattery.

"I presume you are well this night, Miss Wheaton." Mr. Inglis inquired of her as they danced. But before she could answer, he said, "Because your eyes are very lively -- like deep pools of green. They remind me of the leaves on the maples and how they flutter in the summertime breeze, waving their soft hellos to the approaching days. Their beauty can be compared to that of the luscious valleys of the ranging countryside that weave the tender grasses into the fertile grounds."

Mary hesitated, wondering if he was finished with his poetic outburst. She struggled for words as he waited for her response. "Are you a poet, Mr. Inglis?" she warily asked, knowing that probably was not the best thing to say. Proudly, he nodded, sighing as if inspiration hit him right then, and went off on another rambling rant for the remainder of the dance. He now tried to compare Mary's beauty to a summertime breeze, which comes and goes, leaving delight in everyone's hearts, then despair once it had gone.

Mary's next partner was three times her age. Mr. MacDougal was very kind and didn't speak of poetry, which pleased her greatly. However, he told her stories about his grandchildren and his deceased wife, which made her feel somewhat uncomfortable.

"I've got a granddaughter who's just like you," he said to her with a kind smile. "Her nose is like a cherry blossom and her eyes are always so full of life, much unlike Mrs. MacDougal after she had passed."

Mr. Aaron barely spoke two words to her after requesting a dance, but one would expect nothing less from a lawyer. On the other hand, Mr. Smith started a conversation with Mary, although neither he nor the topic interested her.

Finally, after her last dance, she was able to take a break. She sat down to eat with Morgan and the red coat, noting a certain glimmer in her friend's eye, and took great pleasure in the food as she closely listened to the soldier.

"Splendid evening," the red coat said to the women, patting his mouth with a napkin. "It's always nice to have a peaceful diversion from the rigors of life. And the people here are most welcoming. I should come to Denny's Grove more often!"

"It is a pleasant place," Morgan concurred. "It's not far from the moors, and the people are friendly."

"Quite so," the soldier responded. "I'm awfully glad Douglas invited me to attend."

Mary lifted her eyes from her plate and observed how Morgan and the red coat stared at each other, not a word spoken between them. She wanted to learn more about this man.

Placing her napkin gently upon her lap, she asked, "So Mr. Ferzley, how long do you plan to stay here?"

Breaking away from Morgan's eyes, the soldier turned to Mary and replied, "For another week, or at least until my regiment moves again. Colonel Aiden is a very strict man when it comes to relaxing; he can never stay in the same place for more than a short while. But he's a good man and I'm honored to be serving under him." Swallowing another bite, he turned to Morgan and said, "I understand your father was in the militia as well."

"Yes," Morgan replied after a sip of wine, "he was. He served alongside Mary's father and our sheriff, Mr. Adams."

"My father always loved to speak of those times," Mary chimed in. "While the three of them were together, they were quite the troublemakers." Mr. Ferzley grinned mischievously.

"Then military antics are not unique to our generation," he laughed. "All of it's jolly good fun, though."

As he spoke, a cluster of gentlemen and ladies flooded into the dining area, packing the space with their loud conversation and gut-wrenching laughs. Quickly finishing their own meals, Mary, Morgan, and Mr. Ferzley left the room. They drifted to a quieter spot, so that they could continue their conversation without having to shout at each other. Running into a few friends from his regiment, Mr. Ferzley introduced them to the others.

"Men," he said to his friends, "this is Miss Morgan Greenwood and her friend Miss Mary Wheaton." Turning to the girls, he said, "Ladies, this is Hewett Ernest, Jarvis McFerrel, and Hans Kerzlicht. They serve in the same regiment as me."

"How do you do?" all three said in unison. The girls curtsied, seeing that the trio was just as pleasant company as Mr. Ferzley himself, and gladly joined in the conversation without the slightest hint of discomfort.

"Miss Wheaton and Miss Greenwood were just informing me of their fathers' services in the armed forces," Mr. Ferzley told his comrades. "They were trouble-making chaps just like ourselves!"

"Right-o!" Mr. Ernest exclaimed. "I thought the name Wheaton sounded familiar! My father knew your father, Miss Mary." Mary smiled.

"I am not surprised," she responded, "he was quite well-known in the militia, but not exactly for the right reasons."

"Ah, but he's a good man, nonetheless!" Mr. Ernest continued. "He saved the life of one of his comrades in Massachusetts, carrying him for miles before they found their regiment again."

"That would be our sheriff," Morgan interjected. "He and Mr. Wheaton became close friends not long after."

Nodding in remembrance, Mr. Ernest said, "Right, right. Good man. Good man. Is he here?"

There was a slight pause as a worried glance was exchanged between Morgan and Mary. Mary didn't let Mr. Ernest's ignorance bother her, as she calmly replied, "He passed nearly four months ago." It was evident that Mr. Ernest felt terrible for even asking.

"I'm so sorry," he said in all sincerity. "I didn't know."

"It's quite alright," Mary assured him. "He grew very ill this past year and it wasn't expected he would last. But we shan't dwell on that, shall we? Tell me, sir, what was your father's name?"

The conversation continued another fifteen minutes when Mr. Ferzley requested a dance with Morgan. Mr. Ernest and Mary resumed their earlier conversation, when all four soldiers were suddenly called off for important business back at the base camp. Mr. Ferzley was sorry to go, but he was obedient, and said his farewells to the girls, expressing his wish to see Morgan again as soon as possible.

The ball continued, with all its merriment, and with the guests more than willing to stay into the early morning hours. Mary and Morgan sat together playing cards, with no desire to leave the mansion, and talked quietly to each other. As they played, they had memories of Mr. Rodchester interrupting their games. They wished he was there to tell one of his tall tales, or merely wander around their table just to make them uncomfortable. There were plenty of drunkards around today, but it just wasn't the same somehow.

Seeking their amusement elsewhere, the girls strolled into the main room, where the band was playing. They listened to the tunes, and gazed at the throng of dancers on the floor. The group was still going strong after being on their feet for hours, and Mary was exhausted just watching them. But she greatly enjoyed the music and clapped her hands in rhythm.

Hearing the clock strike midnight, Mary stopped to look at it in disbelief. The evening had passed so quickly. She tapped Morgan on her shoulder and pointed to how late it was. She, too, was surprised, feeling that the ball had barely begun. "I'm going to find the water closet. Try and stay out of trouble while I'm gone."

With that, she left Mary. Searching for a bathroom in this mansion would be like going after a needle in a haystack. Mary smiled at the thought, convinced that Morgan would get lost in the great house, and turned to follow her, when she was startled by Nicholas Black. He was still as somber as ever, not reacting in the slightest to her discomfort. He bowed to her, saying, "Miss Wheaton, would you do me the honor of a dance?"

Mary hardly knew what to say before she found herself placing her hand in his as acceptance. He drew her into the line of people preparing for the next song, and stood opposite her with a total lack of emotion.

As the song started, people stared, seeing the undertaker among them. They whispered to one another fearfully as they danced their steps. Mary, however, was more astonished than she was fearful. She saw how his eyes glued themselves to hers, he not breathing a word. Having him stare at her like that put her in an awkward position, forcing her to say something to put her nerves at ease.

"I wouldn't think you one to dance, Mr. Black," Mary said. They moved around each other and met again, and she kept a close eye on him, carefully observing him as he responded.

"Oh?" he said, raising his brows. "And why is that?"

"You seemed too busy to engage in the activity," Mary answered. "What finally broke you?" Pausing for a bit, the two separated, merging with other groups of people in the process, before touching again.

"I thought I'd try something outside of routine," Nicholas finally replied. "And see these lively spirits you claim exist." Mary smiled.

"And your verdict?" she inquired, curious. He allowed her to pass before him to the other side of the line before replying, "I did not think you meant alcohol."

Mary danced a few more steps, studying Nicholas as he spoke to her. While his expression remained unmoved, he was more sociable, yet pleasure, anger, sadness, and a few more emotions jumbled themselves together, forming the undertaker.

The dance ended shortly thereafter and they were plunged into silence. She looked up at him, feeling his eyes pierce hers. Fire burned in his brown irises, yet he was calm, docile, and alluring. She lost herself in those eyes while the people readied themselves for the next song. Suddenly, he bowed to her, breaking her out of her reverie, and turned to leave, passing Morgan on his way out.

Bewildered, Morgan stood next to Mary, staring after Nicholas until he was completely out of sight. Turning to Mary in wonderment, Morgan inquired, "Were you just dancing with the undertaker's son?"

Mary looked at her blankly, then shaking herself back to reality, replied, "Yes." Then, changing the subject, "Were you able to find the toilette?"

Meanwhile, Nicholas was almost out of the mansion when Douglas Rolland and a few of his friends obstructed his exit. "Nicholas!" Mr. Rolland called out to him, trying to be sociable. "It is most certainly a surprise to see you here!" Nicholas simply stared at them, holding his ground.

"It's a surprise to me too," he stated flatly.

Exchanging glances with his friends, Douglas pulled the undertaker towards them, shaking hands with the impassive young man. Then smiling, he continued, "I think I can guess at your intentions for coming." Nicholas shook his head, not knowing what he meant, and drew his hands behind his back, waiting for Mr. Rolland's explanation. He carefully eyed his host, maintaining his solemn demeanor, as Douglas continued, "You were dancing with Miss Mary Wheaton. Trying to woo your way into her fortune?"

"I would never do Miss Wheaton the dishonor," Nicholas replied. Mr. Rolland's friends glared at him, but were taken aback, now seeing the fire in Nicholas' eyes intensify.

The other guests' unease was evident as they stood there, looking over towards their host as if to warn him not to start a conflict with the young Mr. Black. But Mr. Rolland did not catch on, as he continued, "Of course not -- none of us would. But fortune does make an individual appear more handsome."

"When you're blinded by avarice, it does," the undertaker smartly replied. Tipping his hat towards Douglas, he bowed and disappeared into the night, his departure leaving chills behind. Mr. Rolland's friends turned towards him, wondering why he had dared to challenge Nicholas.

"You invited the undertaker's son to your ball?" one spoke up. "Why would you do that?"

"The Blacks rarely if ever speak with anyone in town," another added, "yet they seem to know everything about the lives of every single soul."

"He buried my mother and sister," Mr. Rolland interjected. "I somehow felt indebted to him."

"But that was four years ago," the first pointed out. "So why now?"

"He just hadn't accepted any of my invitations until now," Douglas replied, raising his drink to his lips. "Now I don't have to invite him to anything anymore. Problem solved."

Still, the men stood uneasily, with eyes glancing frequently out the door and into the night. They kept their apprehension to themselves, however, and said nothing more on the matter.

The last party left Scisserioux at the break of dawn. Morgan stayed overnight at Wheaton Manor and the girls slept late into the next day. Dolly would stop by later to learn of all the delicious details.

Chapter Twenty

*I*t was the morning after Mr. Rolland's extravagant ball and Mary had finally risen from her sleep. Dolly brought her breakfast, since she wanted to be the first to learn about the happenings of the night before. Mary's lips had barely touched her toast when Dolly inquired, "How was Mr. Rolland's ball?"

Mary looked at her, calmly placing the toast back onto her plate, and said to her nurse, "Is that why you brought breakfast up to me?"

"More or less," the servant confessed. "But it's also because I knew how exhausted you'd be." Mary raised an eyebrow.

"Fine, fine," Dolly said, dropping her shoulders. "I just desperately want to know what happened. Did you dance with any fine gentlemen? Did any of them make an offer? Answers, dear! Answers!"

But before Mary could say a word, Morgan sleepily shuffled into the room and stood before Dolly. The servant was obviously annoyed. "What's with all the excitement?" Morgan yawned, stretching her arms high over her head. Quickly, Dolly grabbed one of her arms and sat her down on Mary's bed. Now she was wide awake and wondering what the flurry of activity was all about.

"Now then," the nurse said as everyone was situated. "How was your time in Scisserioux?" The girls swapped looks, not particularly interested in making their report.

"It was alright," Mary said, with a hint of irony in her voice. Morgan responded just the same.

"Quite so," she said. "Decent."

"Oh, now I know you're tormenting me!" the nurse cried. "Do tell, please! Before I explode!"

The girls were, therefore, obliged to inform her of every single little detail: the house, the people, the food, the decorations, everything. Morgan told her of the kind red coat she met and Mary's dancing adventures with men whose ages ranged from eighteen to fifty-seven. "And none of them you cared for?" Dolly disappointedly interrupted. Mary glared at her.

"The fifty-seven-year-old was probably the most pleasant to be with," the girl retorted. "I could barely get two words in with Mr. Inglis. Mr. Aaron didn't talk enough, and Mr. Smith was kind, but not my type."

"Ah, but then there's Mr. Ernest," Morgan reminded. "I believe you spoke with him the most." Dolly's interest was suddenly piqued and Mary dropped her head.

"Why did you have to say that, Morgan?" Mary asked her friend. "Now Mrs. Peyton is going to bombard me with thousands of questions regarding him."

And she was right. Dolly plumped down onto Mary's bed and gazed up at her, tossing one question after the other at her with barely a break in-between. She first asked what Mr. Ernest looked like, then what his favorite leisurely activities were, then his hobbies. If any part of Mary's responses were lacking in detail, the nurse was quick to point it out and demand a more satisfying account.

In the end, she was very pleased at what the girl had to say about him. He may not have been rich, but he was a respectable man with a good head on his shoulders, handsome, and strapping. Dolly could see them well-situated and even mouthed the words 'Mary Ernest'. "It does have a certain ring to it," the nurse teased. "Do I hear of any hopes, Miss Wheaton?"

Casually, Mary played with the bedcover and thought about it. "I don't know," she admitted with a shy grin. "He is a wonderful gent and interesting to be sure, but I cannot say that love is factored into the equation. He's missing a key ingredient, but I cannot put my finger to it."

"Well put your finger to it sooner," Dolly urged. "I want to see my little girl married already!" Mary laughed.

"How can you force me to fall in love?" she asked. "It will come when it's supposed to, and you're just going to have to be patient until it does, Dolly!"

The nurse sat up, staring disappointedly out the window. "I presume there wasn't anyone else?" she asked, feeling that her hopes had already been crushed enough, but Mary hesitated.

"Well," she replied quietly, "there was this dance I had with Nicholas Black."

Dolly's head spun around as she peered back at her mistress. Whether she was timid or excited, Mary could not tell. Dolly was, however, very cautious as she cagily inquired, "You danced with the undertaker's son?" Mary nodded.

"Yes," she replied evenly. Dolly shook her head in disbelief.

"He was actually at the ball?" she exclaimed in amazement. "How was it? What was he like?" Mary shrugged.

"It was...nice," she replied, struggling to search for the right words to describe it. "He's very reserved, but also very...witty. He hasn't many facial expressions, though."

"Most of the people there were scared out of their minds," Morgan put in. "I think the dancers next to him and Mary were quick to withdraw, when they got the chance."

Mary pushed aside her tray of food and covers and crawled to the side of the bed where her nurse and friend sat. "How long were you watching us, Morgan?" the girl asked, warily eyeing her.

Morgan hesitated briefly before replying, "A few minutes before the dance had concluded. I had been looking for you amid the crowds of dancers, until I found you and Mr. Black together. I admit, I was staring. But then again, so was everyone else."

Mary, moving herself off of her bed, walked to the window and peeked outside, watching as people aimlessly strolled back and forth. She was unaware of Morgan and Dolly until she chanced to turn their way, and wondered why they were acting so strangely.

"Why are you two staring at me?" she inquired, looking from one to the other. The nurse replied, "Nothing to it." Mary sighed and moved to her closet.

"I'm going to the graveyard to give Papa some new flowers," she declared. "That will give you time enough to discuss whatever it is, without me."

No objections came her way and she finished dressing. Mary went through the garden to pick some lovely flowers before venturing off.

It was a cloudy day and the skies were threatening rain. The streets were crowded with the usual townsfolk, and they waved to Mary as she passed by, cheerfully wishing her a good morning. She returned their greetings and continued down the road, taking in the fresh summer air with delight.

A few people stopped her to strike up a conversation regarding Mr. Rolland's ball the previous night, and the upcoming weddings between Miss Phillips and Mr. Quigley, and Mr. Henderson and Miss Cantwell. But one individual surprised her as he approached.

"Miss Wheaton," Mr. Quinnley called over to her. "Good morning to you!"

"Good morning to you too, sir," Mary cheerily replied. "What brings you here?"

"Just a little something I had to take care of," Quinnley answered. He looked up to check the weather, then back to Mary to ask, "Were you able to get any sleep last night after all the festivities?"

"Yes," she said. "Very good sleep, indeed. And yourself?"

"The same as I do every night," the officer replied. "Although Webster did keep me up a portion of the night with his snoring." Mary smiled.

"That's right," she remembered. "You and Mr. Adams share a residence. I'm just so used to you living with your family in Westwood."

"Yes, well, regardless of sharing a room with a loud companion," Mr. Quinnley went on, "I am eternally grateful to him for taking me on the force. But I rattle on. I saw you at Mr. Rolland's home, but I wasn't able to get a dance, what with all the gentlemen desirous of your time."

"Indeed," Mary replied. "I would have enjoyed the honor. Perhaps the next ball?"

"Right-o!" Quinnley smiled, withdrawing his pocket watch. Seeing what time it was, he tipped his hat again to Mary and said, "Well, I best be off. Mr. Adams is expecting me in town for a civil case. Good day, Miss Wheaton."

Walking on without further interruptions, Mary soon arrived at the graveyard and walked down the row of tombstones. The first one she ran into was Mr. Rodchester's. She placed a few flowers on his grave, and said a few prayers while she touched his epitaph. 'Here lies Barney Duff Rodchester: 1785-1845. A mariner and a friend to all'.

"Oh, Mr. Rodchester," she said to the headstone. "We all miss you so deeply. I think Benny feels the sting of your going most of all, though. He still visits your room and sits on your bed, staring out the window for hours on end. He misses your tales, yes, but mostly he just misses the way you were."

She stroked the stone and kissed it, waving good-bye to it as she next approached her father's plot. When she arrived, though, she saw that fresh flowers had already replaced the old ones. She looked around, wondering who could have done it, but saw no one. Then she noticed dirt being thrown up in the air about a few yards away. Putting her own flowers down, Mary walked over to the hole that the dirt was flinging from, and hesitantly bent down to find Nicholas Black hard at work.

Seeing her shadow, he turned unexpectedly and looked up. Seeing who it was, he greeted her, "Good day, Miss Wheaton. Can I help you?"

Mary swallowed as she said, "I'm not sure. Was anyone in the graveyard before me? I found fresh flowers on my father's grave." Nicholas smiled. This took her aback, since she had never seen much change in his expression.

"His grave looked like they needed new flowers," he replied. Mary shifted her weight.

"You know I come every two weeks to Xavier's to swap out the old ones," she said. "But I thank you for the gesture."

Feeling that nothing more needed to be said, Mary moved on to pay her respects at her father's grave, when Nicholas unexpectedly spoke up. "All alone, I see," continuing to shovel dirt out of the hole.

Mary eyed him before replying, "As you see." Then, curious, she inquired, "Are you at that all alone?"

"That's usually how it goes," he replied nonchalantly. "My father's normally too busy to do it himself -- not that I would make him do it in his old age, of course."

"Is he out making the coffins, then?" she asked. Thrusting his shovel into the ground, Nicholas laid his hands atop it before replying.

"No, Miss; I do all that."

"What about the headstones?" Mary continued. "He's got to carve those." The undertaker looked up.

"Me."

"Tending to the horses?"

"Me. My father can't go near them. He spooks them too easily."

"Well if you do everything, what does *he* do?"

Nicholas smiled, further astonishing her. Jumping out of the hole, he wiped perspiration off his forehead, then looked to her. "Business," he replied simply, moving towards the stable to put away his shovel. She wondered what he meant and followed him. Grabbing two carrots for the horses, he started to feed one to the animal closest to him. He was very gentle with the creature, tenderly brushing through its mane as he fed it, while he handed the second carrot to Mary. "Would you like to feed one?" he asked. Bashfully, Mary reached for the carrot, then looked over to the next horse. "Charlotte won't bite," he assured her. "She's quite tame."

Peering at the animal, Mary fed it while Nicholas rubbed down its muzzle. She petted her, feeling its soft coat through her fingers. Looking back towards Nicholas with a little grin, she said, "You know, you're not as intimidating as everyone says you are." He looked over at her and smiled again.

"Undertakers do stir a bit of uneasy feelings," he admitted, "but that's what happens when no one takes the time to get to know them."

Still brushing through Charlotte's hair, Nicholas' hand suddenly touched Mary's. Looking up, she lost herself in his eyes, observing how they danced into her green. She was about to lock her fingers into his, but suddenly jerked as the clouds above them rumbled. Removing their hands, they broke away from their spell.

"Shall I see you back to the village, Miss Wheaton?" Nicholas politely inquired, not making eye contact with her.

Mary twiddled her fingers, and looking away said, "No thank you, sir. The rain should hold off long enough for me to return home."

She quickly bid him farewell, grasping tightly to her key all the while. She ran past the headstones of Mr. Rodchester and Mr. Wheaton on her way home. Mixed feelings plagued her mind as she left through the front gate of the cemetery, and daring not to look back, she ran like a mad woman to beat out the storm.

Chapter Twenty-One

*N*icholas had barely finished his work when the storm blew in. He was drenched as he ran for shelter, and entered the grounds' workshop to dry off. He wrung out his jacket and hung it on the stand. Letting the water drip from the rim of his hat, he hung it next to his jacket. Disappearing into the next room, he went to change his clothing. When he emerged, he was almost completely dry.

He moved into his workshop area, then lit a candle so he could start measuring a few boards for a coffin he was making. The silence kept him company as he drew lines and numbers on the pieces, doing what he could to keep his thoughts from distracting him. He set each board aside before he grabbed the next one.

The storm outside roared on through these activities. Lightning flashed constantly, and the wind blew with such tremendous force that it violently shook the trees and even tipped over a few of the carriages parked outside. The rushing water was already making some of the roads impassable. Any travelers who valued their lives had hopefully stopped at a nearby inn or taken refuge within some other sturdy structure to wait for the storm to pass.

But Nicholas didn't let it bother him as he sat, stroking his chin, pondering the dimensions of his boards. He rubbed his lips, only half conscious that he was doing so. Shaking himself back to reality, he picked up his pencil and continued to draw lines.

As the numbers crowded his mind, his candle began to flicker, and he sensed a disturbance in his peaceful environment. Without lifting his eyes, he continued his work, wiping the sawdust from his station. "I wouldn't think you'd let a little rain prevent you from doing your work," he muttered, knowing full well who now stood behind him.

There was a pause before he heard a stern reply, "Who says I'm not still on the clock?"

Without moving his head, Nicholas could hear the loud thumps of his father's steps behind him. They did not bother him, though, as he dropped what he was doing and spun around to face him. "Is there something you need, Father?" he asked.

Stepping out from the shadows and into the candlelight, Cairns Black revealed himself and stood silently, letting his eyes explore the area. He was very tall and thin, bald all around, and had a nasty scar that extended from the very top of his head to the bottom of his left eye. His irises were a dull gray, his face flushed of nearly all color; yet he appeared young for his age, since he had absolutely no wrinkles.

A bit ominously, he eyed his son and exhaled. "I've noticed that the violet in the corner of the shop has finally given up the ghost," Mr. Black said. He waited while his son finished a few measurements.

"That's what happens when Death fingers it," Nicholas mumbled as he drew more lines. "Nothing can last forever." Picking up the plank he had been working on, he leaned it against the wall with the others, and wiped his hands. "Alright," he said after a moment, "what did I do this time?"

Cairns stood silently as he placed his hands behind his back, and peered out the window at the storm. He watched as the tree branches fought against the ferocious winds, and sighed. "What makes you assume that you've done something to displease me?" he asked, turning back to his son. Nicholas lifted an eyebrow.

"I assume because when's the last time we've had a decent conversation?" he asked. Cairns did not flinch.

"You're a negative boy, Nicholas."

"I work in a graveyard, Father."

"And a good job you do! The grounds are carefully tended to, the coffins made, and the holes dug. We won't have any funerals for a while, too. What will you do with your free time?"

"I never have free time," the boy responded. "There's always something to do around here."

Nicholas grabbed another piece of wood and started to sand it, hoping that his father would leave him alone. But Cairns was far from moving. "Of course you have free time, son," he replied. "You have the freedom to take a stroll in the orchard, read a book, or go into town for balls, to dance with beautiful, young ladies. Maybe you prefer to woo one of them and exploit her so-called 'charms' for your own selfish reasons…"

"Yes, Father," Nicholas interrupted sarcastically, "because that has been my design from the very beginning." Cairns laughed.

"Oh, you blinded lad!" he cried. "You were this close to giving that girl the 'Kiss of Death'."

"Your derisiveness amuses me, Father. Besides, it's none of your concern. You trusted Mother…"

"May that woman be damned!" Cairns roared, now grasping onto the ends of Nicholas' workspace. "Look where she's got me! Can't you see your thoughtlessness leading you astray?!"

"Can't you see yours?" Nicholas firmly retorted. Mr. Black angrily huffed.

"If I've warned you once, I've warned you a thousand times, Nicholas. Don't get involved with those people!

Now look at what you've done! You've lured in an innocent little girl."

Mr. Black hastily moved away, then stopped. When he had composed himself, he said, "Stay away from her. Whatever means you can use to keep your distance, do it; because you know as well as I what her fate will be."

Nicholas froze, dropped his hands to his sides, clenching his fists in silent anger. He returned to his work. Mr. Black, seeing the look in his son's eyes, said calmly, "Look at me, son. Look at me." Grudgingly, Nicholas obeyed, as his father placed both his hands on his shoulders. Looking deep into his boy's eyes, he said in a more composed manner, "Forgive me, son, for letting my anger get the best of me. But I only want to prevent what happened so long ago from reaching us again. It'll be over before you know it, and you'll forget all about it." He waited for a reply, but none came, as his son simply stared into his eyes. Nicholas waited for his fury to subside before he spoke again.

When he was composed, he said, "Because we both know you forgot about Mother."

Breaking away from his father's grasp, he returned to work, having nothing more to say. Cairns stood and watched him, but kept quiet. He then left, stopping first at the hat stand to retrieve his things. Then, leaning into the storm, he returned to his quarters. They didn't speak to each other for the rest of the day.

Chapter Twenty-Two

*F*or the next couple of days, Mary was out and about, pushing to the back of her mind the dismay which the occurrences of the past months had produced. Dolly noticed the shift in her emotions and wondered as to its cause. However, she refrained from asking questions as she prepared Mary for her dinner with the Greenwoods.

"Do you think it shall rain again today, Dolly?" Mary asked, as the nurse tied her bonnet. "The clouds look a bit threatening, don't they?"

"Aye," the maid agreed, "but the air doesn't speak of it. I believe you're safe for now."

Taking a good look at her, Dolly gently patted the girl's dress, handing Mary her gloves. "Is it just the Greenwoods this time?" the nurse inquired. Mary slapped her hand away.

"Quit fidgeting with the dress," she lightly reprimanded. "It's just fine."

"I found a wrinkle in it, though, Miss," Dolly argued.

Mary replied, "It's alright; it's not like you're preparing me for my wedding day or anything. It's just dinner."

"Yes, but there could be some fine gentlemen at the feast," the nurse pointed out. "Which brings me back to my previous question: Is it just the Greenwoods?" Mary shook her head.

"No," she answered. "I believe the Quigleys might be there, too. And I wouldn't be surprised if Morgan invited Mr. Ferzley. She quite fancied him at the ball." Dolly wiped down her hands and put away her sewing kit, stopping a moment to think.

"Didn't his regiment get called off for important business?" she asked, reaching for a brush.

Mary moved away, raising a finger in the air as a warning for Dolly to back off, before replying, "Perhaps, perhaps not. His commanding officer is the ultimate decider of that. But I best be off. I don't want to be late arriving. I'll inform you of the happenings tonight if I'm not too tired, Dolly."

Leaving the house, Mary climbed into her carriage and drove off to Meadow View Park, the Greenwoods' residence. She looked out the carriage window at the people traveling along the road, and offered her hellos, laughing as some of the children fell over one another trying to outdo their siblings' waves.

It was a cloudy day outside, but the sun broke out briefly and intermittently through the fluffy clouds. Rain did not seem like a threat, which delighted Mary immensely, and she watched as the gentle nudges of the summertime breeze flowed beneath the wings of the birds, sending them high into the sky.

When she arrived at Meadow View Park, she saw all of Morgan's siblings playing games in the yard. Once they caught sight of her carriage, though, they dropped all their things and ran to greet her with joyful shouts of welcome. She had barely stepped out before they were all around her, hugging her and pulling her in towards the house.

"Lillian and Timothy are here!" Harris shouted ecstatically. "Did you know she has a baby in her?!"

"That's nothing!" Wanda broke in, shoving her brother aside. "I lost two of my front teeth this morning. See?"

"I grew this big after we last saw you!" Edgar said with a gesture. "Mama wrote it on the wall. Come see, Miss Mary!"

"Alright, alright," Morgan merrily shouted over to them, emerging from behind. "Let's give Miss Mary some room to breathe before we tell her all your wonderful stories." Turning to her friend, she said, "I'm sorry about the bombardment, but they're always so excited to see you." Mary laughed.

"Oh, it's alright, Morgan," she replied. "You do know how much I love them. 'Tis no trouble at all."

"Off you go now, all of you!" Morgan said to her siblings. "Go wash up for supper."

Obediently, they left, racing each other up the stairs. Morgan led Mary in, taking her things and setting them aside, leading her into the parlor where her family, the Quigleys, and Mr. Ferzley and his friends were seated. Mary, on seeing Mr. Ferzley, restrained a smile, whispering to her friend, "Is Mr. Ferzley still in town or did you somehow prevent him from leaving by kidnapping his commanding officer?"

"Oh hush!" Morgan replied. "His entire regiment is in Denny's Grove indefinitely. I think he rather savors the environment too much to move elsewhere."

"Perhaps because you're here," Mary teased.

Coming further in, Mary was warmly welcomed by Mr. and Mrs. Greenwood and offered a seat near Lillian and Timothy. Hesitantly, Mary extended her hand in greeting to Mrs. Quigley, who turned away and grimaced. Apparently, she had not changed since the wedding. Her husband, on the other hand, was kind and warm with his hello. He smiled and inquired after her health while his wife groaned quietly. He then returned to his discussion about hunting and fishing with Mr. Greenwood. Pandora, Julie, and Cawley frowned at the cheerful atmosphere and complained about it. Lillian and Timothy started their own conversation, and Morgan invited Mary to join her, Mr. Ferzley, and his red coat friends in a game of cards. Agreeably, Mary joined in, and sat between Mr. Ernest and Morgan.

"It is good to see you again so soon, Miss Wheaton," Mr. Ernest said, passing out a few cards to her. "Have you been doing well since the ball?"

"Yes," Mary said, "very well. And how is your colonel?"

"Better than ever," Mr. Kerzlicht chimed in. "We might not be called to war for quite some time!"

"Colonel Aiden's family resides in Denny's Grove," Ernest explained. "He has the date set for departure next week Tuesday."

"Whether he abides by it is another matter," Mr. McFerrel added.

The group continued with their game, listening to the children as they rushed down the stairs into the kitchen, and swapped anecdotes with one another. Quite obviously enjoying themselves, they became exceptionally competitive when Mary won two games in a row. They clearly were the liveliest group in the room compared to the Quigley corner.

"I daresay this is the least favorable thing I'd like to be doing," Cawley whined to his mother. "My Jane yearns for my company and I had to delay our meeting to come here."

"Oh, hush up, Cawley," Mrs. Quigley responded, irritated. "No one wants to hear *your* whining. Think of someone else besides yourself." Turning to her two girls, however, she became a different person. Putting a hand to her head in distress, and falling onto the arm of the couch, she wailed and whimpered about her sorry condition. "Oh how I suffer!" she cried, suddenly rising. "Your sister has made such a fool of herself. Look at her now!"

"It disgusts me to look," Dora replied snobbishly. "Although, Father's companionship with Mr. Greenwood sickens me even more."

"Don't remind me," her mother sulked. "The way he associates with these…people. Insufferable! I swear he wasn't like this when I married him."

"He has fallen from grace to ignorance," Julie scoffed. "Denny's Grove has poisoned his better judgment."

"Forget about your father," Mrs. Quigley said, now settling her nerves. "We've already lost him to the piranhas. Keep your minds clear so you won't fall into destitution, like Lillian."

"I'm marrying a rich woman," Cawley jumped in. "Everything's taken care of, Mother."

"Shut up, Cawley!" Mrs. Quigley snapped. "I don't believe I was speaking to you." Turning away from him, she mumbled, "Lord! You're worse than your father."

Just then the dinner bell rang. That was the cue for Mrs. Quigley and her children to take their leave. She yanked her husband away from Mr. Greenwood, and turning towards Mrs. Greenwood, she expressed her regrets for having to leave so early.

"I'm sure you've slaved over this perfect meal," Mrs. Quigley said, "but we must return home. We are expecting

Chapter Twenty-Two

Cawley's fiancé and her sisters for dinner tonight. My humblest apologies."

Before Mrs. Greenwood could wish her well, Mrs. Quigley was out the door, followed by her three children and her mortified husband. Within a minute, their carriage had pulled away and they were quickly out of sight. Lillian put a hand to her face in embarrassment. "My mother never ceases to amaze me," she whispered to Timothy as they went into the dining room.

The food was very delicious, as always, and the conversation lively. Mrs. Greenwood contented herself in speaking with Lillian during the entire meal, while Timothy spoke with his father about the possibility of fishing over the weekend.

As for Morgan, she lost herself conversing with Mr. Ferzley. She giggled and blushed like a young school girl, and covered a wide variety of topics with him, ranging from family and friends to favorite games and places of interest. Mr. Ernest, Mr. McFerrel, and Mr. Kerzlicht, therefore, spent their time chatting with Mary. It was clear that they all shared the same thought as they observed Morgan and Mr. Ferzley vigorously exchanging stories.

"Herman is not especially discreet in his attempts to win Miss Greenwood's heart," Mr. McFerrel commented, raising a piece of meat to his lips.

Mary eyed the couple, then Mr. McFerrel, and asked, "You really think so, too?"

"Quite so," the soldier continued. "Ever since his friend's ball, he could not shut up about her."

"It's either 'Miss Greenwood this' or 'Miss Greenwood that'," Mr. Kerzlicht put in. "We'd be discussing the positions of infantry, and he'd somehow turn the conversation completely around and begin talking about Miss Morgan again!"

"It's true," Mr. Ernest confessed. "I give him until Tuesday before he completely breaks down."

"Too early," Mr. McFerrel replied. "Perhaps after we return to Denny's Grove."

Mary turned to them, curious as to the meaning of their words, and asked, "What do you mean?" They turned to her, somewhat surprised that she hadn't caught on to what they were talking about.

"We're betting on when Herman will propose to Miss Greenwood," Mr. Ernest said. "It's clear that he will, but the question of when still remains."

Mary had seen some of the signs herself, but to hear this affirmation of her notion from three of Mr. Ferzely's friends was very gratifying. Morgan deserved a good man, too. Too many had come along and broken her heart already, raising her hopes high, only to crush them in the end. For years, she had trouble regaining her trust in the male populace. Only after an exchange of letters with Mary, had she regained the nerve to attend dances again, and speak to various gentlemen that she was acquainted with. Now, she was the heartbreaker, because she refused to let her guard down at even the slightest hint of interest. Unless she was sure of her feelings for a man, she wasn't going to allow herself to float away on his empty promises.

And so, after their meal, Mary and the red coats observed the young couple from a safe distance. Morgan and Herman were too caught up in their own world to worry about the others. The two laughed together even after the family moved outside to walk about the grounds, refusing to break away from one another for even an instant, until Mr. Ferzley took note of the time.

"My friends and I must be off," he said to Morgan in a regretful tone. "The colonel doesn't especially like it when we're out at late hours of the night."

"Then I do not wish to get you into trouble," Morgan replied. "I thank you for coming."

"I thank you for inviting me," the soldier returned. Hesitating for a second, he asked, "May I write to you, Miss?" Morgan was flattered, turning pink with emotion, and nodded.

"I would like that very much."

Happily, Herman grinned and kissed her hand. "I'll write to you the instant we camp in Asia," he promised. Bowing to her, he waved good-bye, then gathered his friends to return to their base.

Morgan sighed as she watched him depart, and moved towards Mary. "Don't think that Mr. Ferzley and I weren't oblivious to you all," she told her. "We might have been deep in discussion, but we would have to be blind if we didn't notice you all staring at us."

"And do you expect anything less?" Mary laughed. "You and Mr. Ferzley are like two puppy dogs, sick with love. Quite entertaining, too."

Slipping past Morgan to sit down, Mary went on. "I approve, nonetheless," she said. "He seems like a reputable chap." Morgan turned to look at her.

"You've been rather cheeky lately," she said to Mary. "Has Cupid struck you with one of his arrows, too?"

"That is none of your concern," Mary replied. Morgan smiled and eagerly moved into the seat next to her.

"Aha!" she exclaimed. "Mr. Ernest has done you in! I knew you could not resist!" Mary shook her head.

"I'm not saying whether he did or did not," she declared. "Either way, my sudden display of impudence is none of your concern."

Morgan tried to extract the secret from her friend, but Mary's lips were sealed. For the rest of the evening, Mary stood her guard, keeping a close eye on Morgan's wiles. Soon enough, Morgan was forced to admit defeat. Bidding her friend farewell as she stepped into her carriage, Morgan returned to her room, wondering what Mary could have meant. The secret bothered her greatly and Mary knew it, yet she delighted in her game of torment. Morgan would find out in due time.

Chapter Twenty-Three

A couple of weeks passed, and Mr. Ferzley's regiment finally departed. Morgan was sad to see him go, but having his letter to look forward to, she waited impatiently, constantly keeping an eye out for the mail. As for Mary, it was time for her to visit her father's grave. She cautiously walked the grounds, avoiding the large mud puddles from the previous day's rain. Then, looking nervously around the grounds, she sat down and addressed the headstone.

"I haven't exactly given you an update on life," Mary admitted, lying her flowers down. "But I shall tell you something that will please you tremendously." Closing her eyes, she listened as her father, standing next to her, gently laid his hand upon his own gravestone. He smiled, then casually placed both hands in his pockets, and raised his eyebrows.

"Oh," he replied, full of curiosity, "and what would that be?" Mary grinned.

"Morgan has fallen in love," she breathed, adjusting her body. "And he's a red coat." Mr. Wheaton laughed.

"You're still a tease," he replied with a little chuckle. "But at least it was Morgan this time, and not you."

"Why, because you refuse to see me married?" Mary asked. Jonathan grinned mischievously and she laughed. "You might have your wish, Papa," she continued. "Does this news please you?"

"In a way, yes; in another, no," he confessed, sitting upon his gravestone. "You're a cautious girl, my Little Rose Petal, which gives me rest; but I also wish to see you happy. There isn't a soul that deserves you, but one man shall stand above the others."

"How will I know, though, Papa?" Mary inquired anxiously. "You knew straight away with Mama, but I am less than certain. Have I met the soul yet?"

But Jonathan didn't reply as he glanced up, gazing out into the field of gravestones behind her. She suddenly opened her eyes; her father had vanished. Turning to look behind her, interested to see what he had been gazing at, she saw nothing but the grasslands of death. Disappointed, she turned, kissed Jonathan Wheaton's headstone, and moved towards the cemetery gate.

As she continued on her way, she came upon Mr. Rodchester's stone. She let her fingers run over the epitaph, then continued to move towards the gate, staring into emptiness. She thought about her father, oblivious to the path she was taking, when she suddenly bumped into Nicholas Black.

"Forgive me, Mr. Black," she apologized, coming out of her daydream. "I didn't see you there." She waited, looking at him, expecting an answer. But he was silent, even though his eyes burned like a thousand infernos. He tightened his grip on his shovel and she recoiled in fear. This was not the same man from weeks earlier.

Swallowing her fear, and trying to appear normal, she asked, "Are you well today, sir?"

"I was, until about a moment ago," he replied harshly. Taken aback by his nasty reply, she reacted in disbelief.

"Excuse me?" she asked, shocked. "Is everything alright?" He only glared at her, tossing his shovel over his shoulder. She wondered about his antagonism and why he was behaving in so discourteous a manner.
She was not going to take this lying down. Returning the stare, she glowered at him and said calmly, "If you wish me to leave, then say so."

He didn't say a word as he stepped aside to allow her to pass through the gate. She turned her eyes away from him and quickly marched down the road to Wheaton Manor.

She was puzzled, wondering why he was being so callous, deliberating the matter while she walked along the dirt path. "Nothing tragic happened," she thought. "Though his voice was very firm when he spoke to me." She continued down the road, letting out an angry groan and continued to ponder. "There has got to be something wrong with him," she said. "No one changes their behavior so quickly without a reason, not unless they're out of their mind."

She arrived home, and not wanting to reflect upon the matter any longer, she ascended the stairs to her room to take a nap. As for Nicholas, after Mary had disappeared from sight, he dropped his shoulders, loosened his grip on the shovel, and frowned glumly. Returning to his workshop, he tossed aside his tools, not caring where they landed, and dropped his head into his hands. Out of the shadows, his father emerged. He was in a tranquil state as he casually approached his son. His eyes sparkled in delight and his mouth curved to form a grin.

He said nothing as he stood there, watching as his son wiped his hand across his face. Nicholas turned his back on Cairns, peering out the window gloomily, as he muttered, "It is finished."

"See," Mr. Black said, "that wasn't so bad now, was it?"

Turning, Nicholas grimly stared at his father but said nothing. Rather, he exhaled heavily and picked up a plank, trying to turn his mind to other matters. Cairns would not leave him, though, as he saw his son's misery. Slowly approaching him, he asked softly, "You trust me, don't you, son?" Nicholas clenched his fist, but nodded.

"Yes, Father," he replied unhappily. Mr. Black looked at his son.

"You'll get over it, in time," he declared.

Nicholas exhaled again, clenching his fist even tighter, and pleaded, "Leave me alone."

Cairns was quick to oblige. Placing his hat on his bare head, he turned and left. Once Nicholas heard the door shut, he let out a sigh and dropped his hands to his sides.

Chapter Twenty-Four

*A*dmittedly, Mary was upset about the events of the preceding day. She, however, carried on with life, putting all discomforting thoughts in the back of her mind. Too much had already upset her and she wasn't going to allow the latest cruelty get in her way.

The days were dull since Dolly's departure for Scotland to visit her sick mother. It was uncertain when she would return, but Mary gave her all the time she needed to get the family's situation back to normal.

In her absence, Mary attended other balls and functions, spending her time with various people, but not particularly enjoying the experience. She continued to visit the graveyard, regardless of Nicholas' attitude, and avoided him whenever she happened to see him. The days passed quickly, but the routine of daily rituals soon began to grate on her nerves. She had to think of something to do before she went insane.

A month after her encounter in the graveyard, and the night before Malcolm and Isabella's wedding, Mary took a little trip into town to celebrate Mr. Rodchester's birthday at one of his favorite taverns: Avery's. She knew she was asking for trouble by going out late at night, but the thought didn't seem to concern her as she strolled into the bar.

Lively music and loud patrons greeted her as she ventured further into the room. Gentlemen were laughing as they dodged around her to pass along drinks to their buddies. A few women drunkenly sang at the piano, sometimes falling over from their tipsiness.

Mary felt very much out of place as she pushed her way to the bar. The bartender, his smile fading, was surprised to see her there as she sat down.

"Mary!" Sylvester shouted above all the din. "What are you doing here?!"

Moving in closer so she could make herself heard, Mary shouted back, "Today's Barney Rodchester's birthday. I thought I would remember him by coming here." The man threw a dish-towel over his shoulder.

"I didn't know you drank," he said. "You didn't come across as the type."

"Oh, I don't," Mary replied, trying to avoid being bumped into. "Do you have any non-alcoholic beverages?" The bartender laughed.

"Water," he said. "That's about it. Hey, why don't you try the rum? Barney loved the stuff."

"He always drank the heavy stuff," Mary noted. "I don't know if I would take to it as well as he did." But Sylvester chuckled, coaxing her to give it a try anyway; reluctantly, Mary agreed.

While Sylvester went off to fetch a glass, Mary nervously sat, tapping her hand against the bar as she scanned the room, looking for a familiar face. She shuddered as she observed how drunkards acted in their natural environment. Some of the people she saw weren't even from Denny's Grove. If they were, the night life was not kind to them. They were loud and obnoxious, scruffy and sweaty, and every few minutes, one would drop to the floor, either from massive drunkenness or a thrown fist. She hoped they would keep their distance from her, because the last thing she wanted was to have to deal with their repulsiveness.

Struggling to stay calm, she turned to her right and found Mr. Adams sitting a few seats away from her. He was by himself, gloomily staring into his mug, and was caught off guard when Mary approached him. "Miss Wheaton!" he exclaimed. "What on earth are you doing here?! You're not by yourself, are you?"

Resting her arms upon the bar, and quite composed, Mary replied, "Everyone worries themselves about my well-being; I'm just fine. But what of you, sir? Are you feeling alright?"

Mr. Adams sighed, casting his eyes around anxiously, and grasped his mug-handle tightly. He took a sip, intently thinking over the question, and turned to her. "That I couldn't say," he replied despondently. Mary sat down next to him.

"What do you mean?" she inquired, worried. "What's wrong?"

But before Mr. Adams could reply, Sylvester slipped a glass of rum in front of Mary and smiled. "Try it, lass," he said with a sparkle in his eye. "And tell me what you think." Hesitantly, she looked up to him, then at the officer, and winced.

Bravely, she took a little sip and had barely swallowed before she let out a cry, "Good Lord! I feel like I just tasted soapy dirt water! How on earth did Rodchester down this?" Sylvester was too busy laughing to answer her question. He gripped his stomach as she disgustedly pushed the drink away.

"Oh, Miss Wheaton!" Sylvester cried, wiping a tear from his eye. "Jolly good show! Capital! Capital! You've gone and given Barney a huge grin from heaven, you did! Ah, but forgive me for not warning you, lass. The spirit is a bitter one, it is."

"That's an understatement," Mary replied, still gagging from the drink. "People who drink this mustn't have the sense of taste."

"Partly true, young miss," Sylvester admitted. "I've gone and lost that sense when I was just a wee lad. My mother wasn't a very good cook. But McCarrier and Rodchester have proven that they savor the stuff. Why? Perhaps it's the buzz that they enjoyed."

Taking the mug from her, the barkeeper gave it to another gent who was waiting to order a drink. Gratefully, he took it and went off to celebrate with a few of his friends in a nearby booth.

"The taste may not be appealing, but the effect of the alcohol makes us forget," Mr. Adams declared solemnly.

Mary stared, seeing that there wasn't much change in the officer's state, and asked him, "What's wrong, sir? Please, you can tell me."

Peering towards her for a moment, Mr. Adams finished his drink. Slamming the mug down on the bar, he stared blankly. "Someone desecrated my wife's grave," he said, forcing the words out of his mouth. Mary was startled. "Cairns Black's son caught two intruders at the cemetery the other night," the officer went on, "digging on the west side of the land. He went to confront them, but the two saw him coming, and ran. The boy managed to tackle one of them, but the man pulled a knife on him and stabbed him. Young Nicholas was alright; he even ran to the stable to fetch his horse to head them off. Unfortunately, he lost them and was riding towards town to inform me of the happenings when he came across Quinnley. Quinnley jumped onto the undertaker's horse, picked me up at home, and brought me to the scene of the crime. I cannot even begin to describe my feelings as I approached that area, Miss Mary. I knew that was where Dorothy was buried. I found four graves desecrated, and peered at the names. My heart sank when I found out hers was one of them."

Absolutely grief-stricken, with tears rolling down his face, Mr. Adams could not finish his story. Mary was quick to comfort him, placing her hand on his, watching as he struggled to contain himself. He was grateful for this, and took in a deep breath, now more composed. His eyes were sad, his face pale, but he was a strong man and restrained himself long enough to say, "They've stolen my wife, Mary, and I don't know where they put her."

Sadly, the girl looked to him, and shook her head. "They'll find her," she declared reassuringly. "Don't you worry, Mr. Adams." The officer smiled, removing his hands from hers, and leaned his elbow on the counter to think.

"You know, it just occurred to me," he said suddenly. "The undertaker's boy was a bloody mess, yet he didn't breathe a word of complaint about it. That wound in his chest was deep enough to kill a man. Still, he went after the goons on his horse, came to locate me, then stood by as Quinnley and I studied the evidence, refusing to see a doctor."

"Have the grave robbers dug elsewhere?" Mary inquired. "Are they looking for something?" The officer shook his head.

"Maybe to make a little profit," he said, "but they're digging all over the cemetery and in a variety of gravesites. They either know what they're looking for, or simply digging up random plots to see what they can find."

He rose up, moving away from the counter. Mary followed him out, unconscious of the looks they got as they left. They were now walking away from town, moving towards Wheaton Manor. Mr. Adams resumed his story.

"Douglas Rolland was not far from the scene," he said. "We asked him if he'd seen the two criminals, but to our dismay, he had not. Quinnley and I have been taking shifts in the cemetery ever since. So far, all is quiet." Mary turned to him.

"How long have these desecrations been occurring?" she asked, still very engrossed in his tale. He paused to think.

"Three or four years," he calculated. "Though it hasn't been until recently that the murders started. Quinnley and I think the diggings and the killings are correlated. It appears that your servant and Mr. Parker may have caught the men off guard. A case of being in 'the wrong place at the wrong time'."

Slowly, Mary's eyes peered heavenwards, and she thought of Rodchester. She wouldn't be surprised if he had caught the grave robbers and threatened to spread their secret. The whole situation was strange and raised so many questions.

She was lost in thought when she was interrupted by Mr. Adams as he turned to Mary, saying, "You Wheatons are always good company. Right now, you remind me so much of Jon. That was a good chap. He's the whole reason I'm alive today. You think a man would never forget about that." Mary gave him a quizzical look.

"What do you mean, sir?" she asked, but Mr. Adams did not reply. Rather, he motioned his hand and declared, "Here you are, Miss; Wheaton Manor." Looking over, she was astonished to find it was so. She should have known he would bring her back to the nest.

She was grateful, curtsying to him before she entered the gate, then turned to go inside. "Don't let your guard down, like I did mine, Miss Wheaton," Mr. Adams called out to her. "Goodnight."

He disappeared in the darkness and Mary locked the gate before returning to her chamber. She fell victim to the sandman's spell not long after.

Chapter Twenty-Five

*W*hen Mary awoke, she knew that the week ahead would be a busy one. Today was the wedding between Malcolm and Isabella, and the following day, Cawley and Jane. Whether she wanted to attend the latter or not depended upon how she was feeling.

Preparing to dress for the day, she searched through her undergarments, yet all she could find were those from the previous day. "Dolly must have mistakenly locked them in her room again," she thought to herself, annoyed. Going out into the hall, she found Miss Landstrom coming out of her chamber and asked her, "Do you have the key to Dolly's room?" The servant girl shook her head.

"Why no, Miss," she responded. "Mr. Kent usually holds her key when she is gone."

Thanking her, Mary went in search of Mr. Kent, running outside the home and into the fields to see if she could spot him. She found him tilling the grounds and planting vegetables. She called out to him and he paused in his work, raising his head to greet her. "Hello, Miss Wheaton," he said with a gentle smile. "What can I do for you?" She was panting by the time she reached him, and returned his smile.

"Goodness!" she exclaimed. "Must be too early for running." She continued, "I'm missing a few of my things and I think Dolly locked them in her room again."

"Things?" the servant repeated. Mary groaned awkwardly.

"You know," she said. "Things."

Finally grasping what she meant, Mr. Kent searched his pockets. "Ah, here it is," he said, handing the key over to her. "But you best be careful. Mrs. Peyton somehow knows if someone was messing with her 'things'." Mary laughed.

"I'll be just fine, sir," she grinned. "Thank you."

Turning, Mary ran back to the manor, ascended the stairs to Dolly's room and inserted the key into the keyhole. She heard a click and exhaled in relief. "He gave me the correct key this time," she whispered in gratitude.

Stepping inside, she peered around, unsure of where she should look first. The room was so neat, probably the tidiest in the house. She went to the closet first, searching through Dolly's assorted wear, making sure that she put things back exactly the way she found them.

"How can anyone live such a tidy life?" Mary wondered, her fingers moving through a few of the folded items. She then searched the trunk by the side of the bed, carefully removing the top items to see if her things were hidden somewhere underneath, but everything was Dolly's.

"Where could she have put them?" Frustrated, Mary walked back to the door, turning to take one final look. Her eyes rested on the chest at the foot of the bed. Without hesitation, she went for it, unlatched it and lifted the top. Inside were a few old dresses and books. Her eyes opened as she picked up a particularly interesting item. Dusting off the cover, she read, "'Property of...Darlene Peyton'?!" Startled, she repeated, "Darlene? I always thought her name was Dolly." Investigating further, Mary found that it was a journal from when Dolly was around her own age.

Guiltily, Mary looked around the room again, hoping that Dolly wouldn't suddenly pop out of the walls and catch her snooping through her personal items. She opened the cover, though she knew she shouldn't, and flicked through several pages before finally stopping. A certain name kept recurring in the writing. Her curiosity piqued, and she continued reading:

'Cardew's family had prearranged a marriage for him -- something I was completely unaware of. I was heartbroken and ran away, marrying a man I knew I couldn't love. But Death got to him not long after, and I was forced to find work in England. I, therefore, took up my living at St. Sebastian's Hospital and cared for a gentleman by the

name of Jonathan Wheaton. One day, he overheard that I was still in search of a job, and straight away offered me a position at his home. Joy wouldn't even begin to describe my feelings as I consented. Walking through those doors into his home, I was overwhelmed. I will never forget the day that I first saw the manor. The grandeur was breathtaking and the decorative aspects spectacular. I often lost myself, not only in the architectural wonders, but also my way around the home. My master, Mr. Jonathan Wheaton, was a kind gentleman, though. He was strongly built, with long brown hair, and his eyes always sparkled with pleasure. He was single, which led me to believe he wanted to marry for love and not for money. Then Mrs. Wheaton came along. Oh, she was a bonnie lass she was! She had great beauty, and her character had the likeness of my master's. I was so fortunate to have met this family, but as good times often do, it all ended on one fateful day...'

It was a stormy April day. Wadsworth tightly latched the door, preventing the storm from reaching the manor's residents, and moved to the back of the house to ensure that the other locks were also well-secured. Mrs. Wheaton was contently rocking in her chair when the servant passed by her. She was blissfully reading when her husband emerged from his study to join her.

He gently kissed her; her hand reached to the back of his neck to pull him down for a longer kiss. He smiled. "Did the baby permit you to sleep today?" he asked. Her book now on her lap, she turned to him.

"For the first time in days," she happily replied. "I didn't know what to do with myself when I woke up feeling so refreshed." Closing her novel, she set it aside, placed both hands under her chin and looked up at her husband. "So," she said in a playful tone of voice, "how are things?" Jonathan turned to her with a smile.

"Things are well," he replied. "Just dealing with the riff-raff of life." Mrs. Wheaton giggled.

"I made you say 'riff-raff'," she delightfully declared. "I just love it when you speak so…British." Mr. Wheaton's smile widened.

"Let me delight you further by saying other British things to you, then, my Pioneer," he said. "Find you any pleasure in the practicality with which I portray my words? It is a capital thing, eh wot?" She laughed again, rubbing her stomach as she felt the baby kick, and let her husband touch her.

Dolly was just then descending the stairs, carrying her linen basket in front of her. Just as she reached the bottom step, Rodchester rushed in from behind her. He obviously startled her, as she dropped her basket, sending its contents flying. She huffed, turning to the young spirit, saying,

"Don't do that to me, Barney. You almost frightened me to the grave!"

But he laughed, tossing the clothes back into the basket, and picked it up. "Whatchye be doin' carryin' this all by yerself, Ms. Peyton?" he inquired, with a twinkle in his eye. Dolly snatched the basket away, and glared at the mariner.

"That's *Mrs.* Peyton, Mr. Rodchester," she corrected. "That means married."

"I see no mister here, lass," the servant joked; Dolly laughed.

"Your attempts to woo me have failed, young mariner," she playfully replied. "Now if you excuse me, I have much work left to be done."

"And I shan't prevent ye from it," Barney said, stepping in Dolly's way, "but I shoold inform ye tha' I took it upon meself to speak wi' some of the sea wrenchin' lads tha' come doon fro' Scotland. One tol' me somethin' interestin'. Apparently, Mr. Peyton's funeral was a sad one it was and that he'll ne'er meet another braw fellow like him again." Dolly slapped him lightly to shut him up.

"Oh, you scallywag!" she angrily whispered.

"Calm yerself, lass," the Scot continued. "I won't be tellin' nothin' to nobody."

He kissed her on the cheek and offered again to take care of the laundry himself. Just then there was a frantic knock on the door. All heads turned, wondering who could be out in such a storm. Dolly went to find out.

Carefully opening the door, she found a man, soaking wet. Mrs. Lou went to fetch some towels for him to dry off, while Mr. and Mrs. Wheaton met with Dolly in the foyer to greet their visitor.

Dolly invited him in, but he just stood there silently, while the rest wondered who he might be. Mrs. Lou returned with the towels, and after he had wiped his face and hair dry, he introduced himself. "Cardew Kent," he said, extending his hand in greeting towards Mr. Wheaton. Jonathan offered his own hand, still curious about Mr. Kent and anxious to find out why he was there. The visitor, now finally dry and relaxed, offered an explanation. "Forgive me for bothering you fine folks," he said to them kindly, "but I was caught off guard by this storm and was forced to seek shelter."

He turned to hand the dripping towel to the servant standing closest to him, and found that it was Dolly. He stopped, staring into her eyes in disbelief, yet amazed that he had finally found her. An instant later, acting as though he didn't know her, he returned to his discussion with the master of the house. Dolly remained dazed through it all.

"You have lovely grounds, sir," Mr. Kent commented, eyeing the home with admiration. "Best take care, though; your stable's becoming a bit musty."

"Is it now?" Mr. Wheaton replied. He thrust his hands into his pockets, studying the man warily, and asked him, "Where do you come from, sir?"

"Edinburgh," Cardew quickly replied. "The edge of the city, actually."

"And you are here because of the storm?" Jonathan asked. Mr. Kent realized there was no pulling the wool over the master's eyes.

"You've caught me, Mr. Wheaton," Cardew smiled. "I've been looking for employment since Scotland didn't meet my fancy."

Slowly, Mr. Wheaton nodded; then turning to his wife he remarked, "You've been wanting that stable repaired for ages." Mrs. Wheaton shook her head.

"Don't plant this on me, Jonathan," she responded coyly. "I don't pass by the wreck and sigh, commenting that it would be grand to rebuild it for the horses' sake."

"I could have sworn you've said something along the way," Mr. Wheaton pushed, but Rosemary stood her ground.

"You may do as you please, my Young Lieutenant," she responded, "but I'm on to your game."

Jonathan grinned, facing the weary traveler again. He stepped forward and studied him from head to toe. He saw that he was a brawny chap, polite, and eager for work and shrugged his shoulders. Without further delay, he asked, "How are you at building structures?"

Cardew grinned, responding, "I've been building since I was a boy, Mr. Wheaton." Jonathan cast an interested look at his wife.

"Well then," he said, coughing into his left hand, "welcome to Wheaton Manor."

Gratefully, Cardew thanked Mr. Wheaton, and Jonathan called, "Dolly, can you please take Mr. Kent to his room?" But she froze, hardly believing what had just happened, and felt a deep pit in her stomach, just imagining what it would be like working under the same roof as he. Mr. Wheaton snapped her out of her daydreaming, though. "Dolly!" he called to her. "Are you alright?" The girl turned toward him and nodded quickly.

"Yes, yes," she replied nervously. "Just fine; forgive me, sir."

She moved up the stairs, without looking towards Cardew. She escorted him to the room next to Mr. and Mrs. Lou's, avoiding any sort of contact with him. He thanked her, but she was quick to withdraw and briskly walked away.

Later that same night, when all the servants and the master and his wife had retired to their chambers, Dolly peeked out of her room and tip-toed downstairs to the kitchen for a piece of bread. Her stomach was aching, since she was too sick to eat anything earlier, and found a little slice of bread out in the open for her to take.

Her tongue barely touched the food before she knew she hadn't the inclination to chew. Rising up, she poured a glass of water and drank it all. She then refilled the glass, sensing the heat surge all over her body, and nearly dropped her glass when Cardew approached her from behind.

"Cardew!" she cried in shock. But he didn't respond as he put both hands to her face and kissed her. Very much caught off guard, Dolly broke away and jumped back in fear. "Stay away from me," she warned. "Just stay away!"

"Why?" Mr. Kent inquired as he recovered her steps. "I've been searching so long for you. I love you Darlene; I've always loved you."

"Not something a married man should say," she responded, angrily withdrawing her hands from his. Cardew shook his head.

"No, my parents wanted me to marry Patrice, but I refused. I wanted to marry you all along, Darlene."

Still, Dolly shook her head from left to right, slowly backing away as her fists clenched, and began to cry. "You refused a little too late," she despondently murmured. She lifted her eyes to him and dried her tears. Then, in a totally different mood, she continued angrily, "You did not stand up for me at all when first confronted by your parents. You stood there like a defenseless ninny, too frightened to oppose their wishes. Well it doesn't matter now, because I'm married:

M-A-R-R-I-E-D. Married, Cardew! Mrs. Darlene Peyton! And there's nothing on God's green earth you can do about it."

Cardew's body grew cold when Dolly was done speaking, even as her eyes burned like firestorms. He felt the silence mocking him as he stood there, gazing into the eyes of the woman he loved. His head dropped to his chest in defeat and exhaling heavily, he muttered, "I've come too late, then. Another man has swept your heart right through my fingers when I knew I could have prevented it all along. I am such a fool! But the man who possesses your heart is a blessed soul. I want nothing more than your happiness, Miss…Mrs. Peyton."

He then bowed, gloomily ascending the stairs to his room, while Dolly kept her ground. She put a hand to her chest, sensing the bitterness building up. Her eyes were tearing up again.

She presumed he would leave the very next morning, but Mr. Kent kept his word to Mr. Wheaton and rebuilt the stable. It was a while before the two returned to speaking terms, but their words were not of endearment or love.

'…I know I could have easily informed him of the great passion that burned in my heart, and how I never stopped loving him and that I wasn't married. But I was a pride-filled, little girl. The pain produced by his idleness and that kiss to Miss McGreggor's face lingers in me to this

very day. But one pain stands far greater than these -- one I shall never speak of. I blame myself entirely for never having a happy life and I don't seek to deny it. I never spoke to anyone of my pain nor will I ever. When I am ready, I will face him. As for now, I will live with the fate I have chosen'.

Mary set the journal down, thinking how amazing it was that Dolly had lived such a past, and had not breathed a word about it to anyone. She was always a private person, never wishing to bring back a past which haunted her to this very day, and now, Mary understood why. "Dolly's not married," she said to herself in shock. "And she was in love with Mr. Kent!"

But all these thoughts were set aside when a voice startled her from behind. "Did you find what you were looking for, Miss Wheaton?" Mr. Kent called from the doorway. Throwing the book behind her back and swishing her body around, Mary quickly closed the trunk.

"They are not here," she quickly responded. "She must have put them elsewhere."

Rising to her feet, she walked past Mr. Kent, still trying to hide the book from him. But he plucked it right out of her fingers and inquired, "What do we have here, Miss Rosemary?"

"'Tis nothing," Mary replied nervously. "Just a book."

The servant eyed her, then the manuscript, and said, "This reads 'Property of Darlene Peyton'. Last time I checked, you were not Darlene. What are you doing with this, and why were you prying in places you shouldn't have been?" Mary was anxious, seeing that she was caught in the act of snooping, yet she calmly composed herself, remembering what she had read in the journal.

Her eyes rose to meet Mr. Kent's as he patiently waited for an answer. She replied coyly, "I don't know, Cardew; you tell me."

It was evident that she had struck a nerve. The servant swallowed nervously. "Don't read this," he said to her quietly, as he proceeded to return the journal inside the nurse's trunk.

Mary's heart sank. She could see that he wanted very much to read the journal's contents, but he loved Dolly too much to betray her trust. He latched the trunk and went to exit, when Mary whispered to him, "She's not married, you know."

He stopped. Turning to Mary, he looked into her eyes to see whether her words might be true. He could clearly see that it was so. Slowly, he continued down the hall and returned to his own room without another word.

Chapter Twenty-Six

*S*ummer was nearing its end by the time Mr. and Mrs. Henderson and Mr. and Mrs. Quigley had wed. Mary, who had decided to attend both wedding ceremonies, watched the differences between the couples in how they stood and looked at one another before the altar. Malcolm and Isabella were clearly in love, because every time the priest was not addressing them, they would be looking at each other in the enchantment of the moment. Isabella whispered a few times to Malcolm during the priest's sermon, and there was no wiping the smiles from their faces. A week after they had tied the knot, they visited Mary at Wheaton Manor to thank her for all her help.

"Malcolm told me of the conversation you two had the day Mr. York and I first saw you," Isabella said. "I was very much caught off guard when Malcolm proposed to me that very night, but I now know whom to thank."

"Mrs. Henderson also came to me the night you two had that chat at Harlow's," Malcolm chimed in. "I suppose we have the same counselor whenever we need to talk. A big thank you to you, Miss Wheaton. You've made us the happiest couple on the planet."

As for Cawley and Jane, they stood up at the altar and wouldn't even look at one another. Both of them scowled as they exchanged their vows, and Jane yelled at the priest for prattling on too long about children and love. If Mary hadn't expected to see a show, she probably wouldn't have gone.

Eliza Orchid, Jane's closest friend, was both devastated and enthralled, often switching between the two emotions. "I am so happy on *your* account," Eliza said to Jane. "Mr. Quigley is a rich and handsome man to be sure! But what shall I do without you?"

"I don't know," Jane replied snobbishly. "I'm a married woman now -- a richly married woman -- and I have my wifely duties to fulfill. But don't fret, darling; you'll find someone."

The elder Mrs. Quigley was ecstatic over the fact that her son had married a wealthy woman, but her husband was less than enthusiastic about his new daughter-in-law. Jane barely spoke to him, and when she did, it was obvious that her civility was faked. Pandora and Julie got along just fine with her, though Jane still considered them children, and spent as little time with them as possible.

The drunkards were still drunkards, the religious still pious, and Mary was still Mary. Nothing had changed, as far as Mary was concerned, with one difference: Dolly's absence. If she ever wanted to get back into her nurse's room, she would have to either steal the key from Mr. Kent or climb up the side of the house and through the window. She, therefore, settled down in the study to continue with the reading of her parents' letters. After months of poring over them, sadly she was now down to the last two letters. She carefully opened them, trying to savor the moment as long as she could, and read her father's letter first.

My dearest Rosemary,

I'm finally coming home, after two years of service. The Americans had the home advantage all along and, as I expected, we were driven out and back to our land. We admit defeat, yes, but some of the men are too stubborn to leave the land. Many of them are in Canadian forts or other surrounding areas, but it doesn't seem too promising. My side has been better, but I am grateful to be alive. I cannot wait until I see you in London, my Pioneer. I have news that is so immense that mere paper cannot contain it. God bless and good health, Love.

Yours truly,
Jonathan Wheaton

My Young Lieutenant,

I was so happy to hear of your coming home. Things have been rather gray without you. And though you have come to visit me whenever you've had the chance, I will be overjoyed at seeing you whenever I please. Father's looking to finish that card game you two had begun on your first meeting and Mama is sewing up a storm for you. I hope you like sweaters, because you're going to be wearing them until you die. I'm counting down the days until your return. Be safe, my love.

Yours,
Rosemary Smith

"That's it?" Mary said to herself in disappointment. "But the letters were so short! I would think that they would write longer…" Her thoughts trailed off when a small note fell out of her mother's letter. She picked it up, and quickly realized that it was from her father to her.

My little Rosemary,

I can sense how disappointed you are in finishing these letters, especially considering your mother's and my last letters were very short. There is a reason for that. When I first started to write to your mother, the letters were longer and more personal, which I enjoyed very much. But one day, one of my letters got into the hands of my commanding officer and he wasn't very happy to read what I had to say about the enemy. I was supporting them, to state it plainly, and thereafter he monitored every letter I wrote back to your mother. My regiment supervised me for the rest of my service period to ensure that I wasn't sneaking away and giving information to the enemy. But the rank and file who made up that regiment knew me better, and was able to smuggle some longer letters back to England. Your mother never questioned me, though I think she knew I had got into trouble somewhere along the way. But I'll tell you this, Rosemary: your mother was the most beautiful woman I have ever laid eyes on. Her kindness radiated to her outer beauty and her occasional sarcasm constantly silenced my own attempts. Mere words do not do her justice, but I want you to know how wonderful she really and truly was. As for you, my dearest Rosemary, no man could ever deserve your heart. You are of your mother's upbringing and the fact that I was able to secure her surprised me vastly. I probably should have mentioned this earlier and I hope I am not too late, but I did bequeath a specific duty to a close friend of mine: Sergeant Webster Adams. I gave him the most important duty of all: to give his consent to the man who asks for your hand in marriage. I trust you, to be sure, but I want you to know that you haven't lost me. You are my most precious gift in the world and Webster is my connection to you. This is my last letter, my Little Rose Petal. It is ultimately up to you what you would like to do with these writings. I love you more than you could ever imagine and I'll always be watching, so be careful!

Love always,
Papa

Chapter Twenty-Seven

"*I*'m glad you could come for a visit, Mary," Morgan said to her as they settled under a large elm in the Park. "I haven't seen you since Mr. Henderson's wedding."

"Well, with festivities subsiding, I'm grateful for the time I do have," Mary replied.

September had arrived and already England was showing signs of autumn. The trees were beginning to change colors and the air was turning cool. The Grove was best seen at this time of year, but the season seemed to fly by so quickly. Uncharacteristically, the country had recently been experiencing a string of sunny days which made the people much more sociable than they normally were.

Now sipping tea with Morgan, who appeared to be lost in a letter she had just received, Mary watched as the sun danced behind the clouds, allowing streaks of light to peek through the little holes of white cotton. She took it all in with great ease, letting her ears relish each sound of nature as she closed her eyes to listen. She felt more relaxed than she had in ages.

"Do you ever just sit outside and think how different nature is, compared to our man-made environment?" Mary asked, as a gust of wind swept through her hair. Morgan, who had been engrossed in her letter, now looked up.

"Oh, yes," she said, though she hadn't been paying attention to Mary. Mary took another sip of tea.

"And how Edgar fell into a well, and Timothy and his wife became fugitives?" Mary teased, knowing full well that Morgan's mind was elsewhere.

"Strange, yes," Morgan mumbled, as her eyes continued to scan the note. Mary laughed.

"Oh you lovesick puppy!" she cried. "Just read me the letter before any more of your siblings are assigned fates."

Morgan turned towards Mary. "Oh, no, no, no!" she quickly replied. "I'm so sorry. I did not mean to be so unsociable."

"The letter's from Mr. Ferzley, isn't it?" Mary guessed. Morgan's face flushed pink. She was about to disagree, but thought better of it.

Readjusting herself in her chair, she replied joyfully, "Oh Mary, this is the first time I have ever received a letter from any gentleman other than my father. I am all in raptures and I cannot help but think he fancies me."

"Of course he does!" Mary responded. "At Mr. Rolland's ball, he was hesitant to even leave with his company. He continued to look back towards you before exiting through the door. *And,* at the family gathering in July, he couldn't stop talking to you." Morgan's smile grew wider.

"He *is* such a fine gentleman," she said as she fidgeted with her fingers. "I have never met anyone quite like him. He's so intelligent, yet he speaks so deceptively plain. I don't know, Mary. Maybe it's too soon to say, but I think I love him."

Morgan lightly exhaled and peered up to the clouds, now absent of all reality, and beamed. Mary smirked. "Why don't you read the letter to me?" she asked.

Morgan picked it up. "I'll read you a little excerpt," she said, and began:

'...Asia is such a mesmerizing land, filled with unfathomable possibilities. The moment we made a crossing into the territory, it was as if we were venturing into a completely different realm. The people dress and speak so differently that I'm surprised we belong to the same world. Their customs, though strange, I have learned to cope with. The food, not so much. As for our men, we lose a few every day, but results seem promising in our favor...'

"He goes on to talk about their enemies and allies, whose names I can barely pronounce," Morgan said, "but he is doing well and expects to return by the end of the year."

"He's in the Punjab Empire, right?" Mary asked. Morgan shrugged her shoulders.

"I don't know," she confessed, "but that sounds about right. The Muslims are giving them a hard time."

Stuffing the letter back into the envelope, Morgan set it aside and took a sip of tea. "I've been taking all room for words," she said, placing the cup on the saucer. "Tell me, how have you been?"

Mary reached for her tea before replying, "I've been well enough. Outdoors has been very stimulating to my senses, and I feel very calm and relaxed."

"And what of Dolly?" asked Morgan. "Is she still trying to persuade you into matrimony?"

"She can persuade all she wants, but without a man, her urgings have been met by silence." Morgan chuckled.

"Who has she suggested thus far?" she asked. Mary moved to the edge of her seat.

"Well, let's see," she said, eyes gazing upwards in thought. "Mr. Hearn, Mr. Henderson, Mr. Rolland, Mr. Quinnley, Mr. Ernest, and basically all the other eligible bachelors in Denny's Grove."

"Widowers, too?" Morgan offered; Mary rolled her eyes.

"Anyone who's single," she responded. "You can imagine that I somewhat enjoy her absence, because I can actually leave through the door without her shouting after me to keep my eyes peeled." Morgan raised her head.

"Oh," she said, "Dolly's in Scotland? What on earth is she doing there?"

"Her mother hasn't been doing too well," Mary explained. "Doctors gave word that she was not going to last past September, so Dolly went directly to her. I don't know when she might return, but I offered her as much time as she needed to be away. She has a large family, too. I believe it's six brothers and seven sisters."

"Good Lord!" Morgan exclaimed. "And all of them survived?"

"No, I think there were eighteen altogether," Mary replied, "but three of them were miscarriages and the other three were infected with some nasty disease. Dolly has not seen any of them since leaving Scotland nearly thirty years ago."

"Wow," Morgan exclaimed. "And how old is she now?" Mary thought for a moment.

"Forty-six," she replied. "And still a young spirit, I might add."

At age seventeen, Dolly married; but, as Mary had read in her journal, her husband had died not long after. She was nineteen when she came to work for Jonathan Wheaton. If only Mary could capture Dolly's story in its entirety. A few pages of her journal had revealed so much; imagine what a hundred pages might yield!

And though Mary ached to tell her friend the secrets she withheld, she kept them to herself. One secret, however, would be more difficult to keep as Mr. Ernest's letter lingered on Mary's dresser at Wheaton Manor.

Chapter Twenty-Eight

A week after her visit with Morgan, Mary and Wheaton Manor welcomed Dolly home with open arms. She was grateful to be back too, after having taken care of so many things back in Scotland. She hugged Mary and inquired about the events that had occurred while she was away.

"Nothing special to report," Mary replied, holding her breath. She watched as Dolly took off her gloves and bonnet.

"And how is your family?" Mary continued, guardedly. Dolly sat down, pausing a moment before replying.

"It was so nice to see them all again," she replied with a heavy heart. "It's been too long."

"How was your mother?" Mary went on. "Did she go peacefully?"

"I would have to say so," Dolly replied calmly. "I was next to her when she breathed her last. But she was prepared to go; she knew it was her time. I only wish I could be half the woman she was. What a saint! At least she's able to see my father again."

"Who all were there?" Mary asked. "All your siblings?"

"Yes, yes," Dolly said, "all eleven of them."

"And Mr. Peyton?"

"What?"

"Was Mr. Peyton there?" Mary asked cautiously.

She could see the anxiety in her nurse's eyes as she searched for an answer. Dolly readjusted herself in her chair and looked hesitantly at Mary. "Yes," she replied finally, "he was there." Mary's heart dropped, but she continued her questioning.

"And did he talk to you?" Dolly nodded.

"Yes," said the nurse, "he told me he loved and missed me."

Mary was not satisfied as she persisted. "What were his words exactly?"

Now her nurse grew apprehensive. She started to say something, then thought better of it.

"I'm very tired, dear," Dolly said at length. "I'll tell you later. Right now, I must seek out Mr. Kent and get my key back from him."

Dolly went out into the fields and found Mr. Kent building a new chicken coop. Mary followed discreetly, and watched Dolly's meeting with Cardew Kent from a safe distance.

"Mr. Kent," Dolly called out to him. The servant did not acknowledge her, and carried on with his work. "Mr. Kent," Dolly tried again. Still no response. "Cardew!" she shouted.

This time, his head popped up, and in an irritated tone, he asked, "What?"

"I need the key to get into my room," Dolly replied. "May I have it?"

Glaring at her, Mr. Kent set aside his tools and searched his pockets. Withdrawing a ring of keys, he handed her a key and went directly back to work. She was greatly troubled by his behavior and asked if anything was wrong. "Why would there be?" Mr. Kent responded sharply. Dolly was taken aback.

"Are you sure everything's alright?" she persisted. "Did anything happen while I was gone?" Turning around, Mr. Kent dropped his tools and stood up.

"No, of course not, Mrs. Peyton," he almost snarled. "How is your husband?" Dolly looked at him awkwardly.

"Fine," she declared. Then she took another long look at him. "I think you need to get out of the sun, Mr. Kent. It might be affecting you."

"Oh, no; I'm fine," he replied in the same tone of voice. "I would never lie about my well-being. In fact, I would never lie. Lying is such a terrible thing. Anyone who does lie mustn't have any scruples at all. Don't you agree, Mrs. Peyton?"

"I suppose so," Dolly replied uncomfortably. "Did you eat some bad bread or hit your head on something?"

The servant reached for his tools as he answered, "No, but I wish I had!"

Without another word, Cardew returned to his work, leaving Dolly in a whirlwind of confusion. She shook herself of it, though, as she returned to her room for some much-needed rest.

Mary watched her leave, then turned her attention to Mr. Kent who was now feeling the impact of the earlier exchange. Gently, Mary placed a hand on his shoulder and inquired, "Are you alright, Mr. Kent?" There was a long pause before he responded.

"You shouldn't have told me what you did, Miss Wheaton," he replied sadly. "Now I'll wonder every time whether Darlene is truthful in her words."

Quietly, he returned to his work while Mary went back to the house. As she was climbing the stairs to her room, suddenly she heard a knock on the front door. Since there was no one else around to answer it, Mary opened it herself. It was Mr. Winkleman. He tipped his hat towards her in greeting, and inquired if he could impose on her time for a moment or two. Readily, Mary invited him inside and he took off his hat. In his other hand, he held a small metal box. Mary offered him a seat, noticing that he looked a bit tired, but he declined, assuring her that he should be leaving in a few minutes.

"It is good to see you," Mary continued. "To what do I owe the pleasure?"

Mr. Winkleman handed the box to Mary. She looked at it, puzzled, as he explained, "I was cleaning out Louis's office and I found it in his desk drawer. I believe it was your mother's."

Opening it, Mary found a silver watch inside, with a personalized inscription from her father to her mother: 'With all my love, Jonathan Wheaton'. She smiled, looking at her visitor as he continued, "Louis hid so many things around his office; he wasn't exactly the most tidy individual. He had so many documents and miscellaneous objects around his office that it took me months to clean it out. But he was such a good man. God rest his soul."

Mary smiled, put the watch back inside the box, and set it aside. "How does Mrs. Parker fare," she asked. The banker shrugged.

"She's beginning to fade, I'm afraid," he replied, sadly. "Ever since the funeral, she's been confined at home. I've been doing all I can to persuade her to venture out of doors, but she refuses. She still remains the same gentle woman, though." Mary nodded her head sympathetically.

"My prayers go out to her," she said in all earnestness. "You are so generous to care for her."

"Don't pull that on me, Miss Wheaton," Mr. Winkleman chuckled. "The Parkers have given me a life and it's the absolute *least* I can do for them. I only wish there was more I *could* do."

"The little you do adds up over time," Mary told him. "But I thank you for taking the time to bring this to me."

"It was no trouble at all, Miss Wheaton," said the banker. "You were on my way to the Songbird Village anyway."

Leading him out, Mary opened the door for him before he remembered something. "Oh, and Miss Wheaton," he said. "If there's ever anything you need, don't hesitate to call upon me."

"I promise," Mary assured. "Good day, Mr. Winkleman."

Mary stood there a while, watching as Mr. Winkleman disappeared around the curve in the road. She then retraced her steps to the staircase and entered her room. So much had happened so quickly. Her time in Denny's Grove had not been pleasant at all. She was seriously contemplating returning to the Wellington's. But her train of thought was cut short as the sound of a fiddle rose from the graveyard.

Chapter Twenty-Nine

*I*t was already that time again for Mary to set flowers by her father's grave, yet she could not get to it this morning. Timothy and Lillian had paid an unexpected visit to the manor, which Mary always welcomed.

They appeared to be in good health, as always. Lillian's belly had grown larger since the last time Mary had seen her. Timothy had hardly changed, save for the few shimmers of gray in his hair.

Entering the parlor, the two apologized. "We are so sorry for dropping in like this," Lillian said as she took a seat, "but Timothy and I wanted to see you before we departed for the north."

"Are you moving?" Mary inquired, worried. Timothy nodded.

"My employer wishes me to move closer to the factory," he said. "There's already a home waiting for us."

"Gives me the chills a bit," Lillian added, "because it's in Scotland."

"Not in Ayr, though," Timothy broke in, "so I believe we're safe from any Rodchesters."

"He lived in Arran," Mary clarified. Timothy paused for a moment.

"Oh God, I'm in trouble," he joked.

For the next few minutes, the three exchanged stories and laughed, feeling all the while, in the pit of their stomachs, the sorrow of parting. Mary was saddened most of all, because Timothy was one of her closest friends. It was painful to think of him moving so far away. They had all thought that their families would be together forever, but reality was turning out differently for the Greenwoods and the Wheatons.

Very shortly, the visitors rose to leave, bidding farewell to Mary for the last time, and wishing her well. "Come and visit us, Mary," Lillian said. "It would be so good to see you on the earliest convenience."

"I will," Mary replied, and hugged her. Bidding Timothy good-bye was much more difficult, as a single tear rolled down Mary's face. Timothy, too, was upset, but he smiled through his sadness and assured her that everything was going to be just fine.

"We had some wonderful adventures, eh, Mary?" he said, bravely trying to stay composed. "I'll miss you so much."

They embraced, and Mary cried a bit on his shoulder. "I wish you didn't have to go," she said. "Life will be gray without you." But he put a hand to her face and gently kissed her on the cheek, while still holding her in his arms.

"Remember how we used to play in the graveyard?" he reminded her. "And we said that we would always be friends."

"Always," the Wheaton girl breathed. "That's what the etching on the tree was for."

"Right," Timothy said. "Our adventures are only beginning, Mary. Life will change, but that's how it always has been. You'll meet some nice gentleman and forget all about me." Slowly, Mary lifted her head and stared into his eyes.

"Impossible," she said, and they hugged again.

Not long after, the Greenwoods departed for the north. Mary sat on the landing, gazing sadly as their carriage pulled away from Wheaton Manor. Things were changing awfully fast all around her, yet she had tried to remain constant through it all. She felt like she was trapped in the past, with no one to throw her a line to help her escape. Perhaps it *was* time to leave Denny's Grove. At least when she was in Osiris Creek, time moved with her. The Wellingtons were kind people, and she now missed them.

But this was a big decision for her. She needed to consult a higher power. Since Dolly was unavailable, she went to the graveyard to pray about her situation in the church. She entered the church cautiously, peeking in to make sure that she was the only person in there. Two candles were lit at the altar, as always. The place was empty.

Gratefully, she walked in and kneeled at one of the front pews. She remained there for a long time, contemplating what she should do. The shadows stretched around her, and soon the daylight faded and the moon came out. She gazed up at the cross above the tabernacle, tightly squeezing her hands together in prayer. "Father in Heaven," she whispered. "Please give me a sign of what I should do. I am so confused, and I trust in no other judgment beside Yours. Help my disbelief and strengthen my belief. Erase all doubt and help me make the right choice. Let Thy will be done."

She rose, making the sign of the cross before genuflecting, and moved towards the exit. She could feel autumn closing in. A cold breeze chilled her, forcing her to cling tightly to her cloak before it blew away. She carefully followed the path to the front gate, occasionally stumbling on unseen objects, until she could make out the St. Xavier's Cemetery sign ahead of her.

Before she was able to proceed any further, however, something startled her and she jumped, thinking it was Nicholas Black. But then she heard a voice, and realized that it was not. "Miss Wheaton!" the voice cried out. "What are you doing here?" Squinting intently at the man's face, she saw that it was only Mr. Quinnley, and sighed in relief.

"Oh, Mr. Quinnley," she said, grasping at her heart, "you frightened me." Nervously, Quinnley looked around the grounds, then at Mary, and roughly pushed her behind a tree.

"What are you doing here so late at night, Miss Wheaton?" he repeated. "It's dangerous."

"I was in the chapel," Mary explained. "I did not expect to be out so late at night."

"You have to get out of here," Quinnley declared. "Mr. Adams and I believe we have located the grave robbers."

But before Mary could leave, a tall man, dressed all in black and carrying a shovel, walked in from behind Quinnley. "Come on, Norbert," the voice said. "We have to loosen the north side."

Mary stepped back in fear as Quinnley yelled to the man in irritation. "You idiot! Does it look like I'm alone?" Looking past the officer, Mary could see that the second man was Mr. Winkleman, her financial advisor.

Mr. Winkleman lowered his shovel and stared at her. "I fear I have come at the wrong time," Mary whimpered. A bit annoyed, Quinnley drew his hand gun and pointed it at her. He retrieved a second gun, which he handed over to Winkleman, watching Mary all the while.

"Looks like we're going to have to get rid of this one, too, Tom," the officer said, and Mary's heart sank into her stomach.

"It was you two," she gasped. "It was you two all along. But why?" The men exchanged glances, and glared at her, clinging tightly to their weapons. Mary looked around, spied a knife in Winkleman's buckle, then looked back into the barrels of the two guns.

But the two explained themselves, figuring that it couldn't hurt since they were going to kill her in any case. But first, they scanned the grounds, just in case anyone might come to the Wheaton girl's aid. Quinnley was the first to speak. "Mary, do you know what's underneath this graveyard?" The girl shook her head, and Quinnley smiled. "A diamond mine. More diamonds than you could ever imagine. That brainless undertaker only had to dig a few more feet and he would have discovered it."

"Norbert found it by accident when he was surveying the moors," Winkleman interjected. "He discovered a cave that led to a mine, running all the way under the graveyard. Some of the largest diamonds could only be loosened from above."

"But why did you kill Mr. Parker and my servant Rodchester?" Mary interrupted. They both laughed, remembering well the situations, and proceeded to enlighten her.

"I went to the bank with the diamonds," Quinnley explained, "and Tom here was working at the time. He inquired how I got them, and I told him."

"I threatened Adams on him..."

"And I agreed to cut him in for some of the profit if he kept quiet."

"We worked under wraps for years, until Parker found one of the deposit boxes full of diamonds. I did the only logical thing and killed him, then called Quinnley over to cover up the crime scene."

"As for your servant," Norbert said, "he overheard us arguing in an alley following Parker's death. Remember the hole from when we were kids, Mary? The one under the bush?" Mary nodded, knowing exactly what he meant.

"You used it to get into his room," she deduced, now realizing another crucial detail of the case. "You dressed like the undertaker and his son to plant the blame on them."

"Oh yes," Quinnley replied, diabolically. "We were careful to let at least one witness see us dressed like the Blacks. The fact that Douglas Rolland was close by during both murders only added to the brilliance of it all."

"And you dug in broad daylight, too," Mary guessed, "where no one would ever question you. Now that I think about it, though, only the young Mr. Black dug the graves."

"Nobody seemed to notice," Winkleman laughed. "Everyone's too scared to confront them!"

Mary fell back, sickened by how Quinnley and Winkleman took pleasure in their work. Mr. Parker had been like a father to Winkleman, yet had been killed without any compunction whatsoever. And Rodchester! Talk about being in the wrong place at the wrong time! If he had only sought help, perhaps he would be alive today. But he had always been a cautious man, and Mary figured he did not wish to endanger any lives, except possibly his own.

The stealth, lies, and deceit that the two had gone through, just to mine the diamonds, was astounding. But Mary was more fearful for her life now. She knew that they would have to kill her, but how they were going to do it was less clear.

Mary's fate rested in the hands of the two murderers. Disturbingly, Quinnley smiled as he calmly advanced towards her. "Too bad we'll have to dispose of you too, Miss Mary Wheaton," he sneered. "I was growing quite fond of you."

Suddenly, everything went black for Mary. The next thing she knew, she was trapped in a dark space, with a massive pain in her head. She tried to get up, but was constrained on all sides. She frantically searched for a way out, but there was none. Mr. Quinnley and Mr. Winkleman had buried her alive in a coffin.

She was scared; she knew she was going to die. The air within the coffin was depleting. With tears streaming down her face, she prayed, "Oh Lord, please save me, but not as I will, but as You will."

Thoughts of her friends in Denny's Grove raced through her mind. All hopes of visiting Timothy and Lillian in Scotland, or attending Morgan's wedding, or seeing herself at the altar, were now shattered. She was an innocent soul trapped in a cruel world, and she would suffer for it.

"The fiddle wailed for me," she muttered gloomily, remembering Rodchester's warning. "That tune was so melodic, and the notes so unearthly. Oh, he must be reprimanding me for not listening to him!"

Fate was closing in on Rosemary and she could feel hopelessness seeping into her veins. She tried pushing the top off the coffin, but she was literally six feet under the ground, and it would not budge. A cold sweat poured over her, and after about the twentieth attempt, she gave up. It was no use; she would be dead by morning.

Mary was forced to accept things as they were. She calmed her nerves and rested her folded hands on her stomach. Closing her eyes, she let the songs of Death put her to sleep. No more did thoughts about family bother her, no more did worries about life plague her mind. She kept still, and waited for Death to take her.

Before she took her last breath, she felt the earth shake from above. She gasped, wondering what was happening, when the lid of the coffin was removed. She immediately sat up, gulping in the fresh air. Turning her head, she discovered that her rescuer was none other than Nicholas Black.

Filled with relief, she sprang into his arms and cried, "Oh Nicholas! Thank you! Thank you, Nicholas!" She didn't care that this was the man who had earlier spoken so rudely to her. She was just so grateful to be alive.

He clung to her in a tight embrace. Finally releasing her, he asked, "Who did this to you?"

"It was Mr. Quinnley and Mr. Winkleman!" she panted. "They killed Mr. Parker and Rodchester, and threw me in this hole!"

Assisting her out of the ground, Nicholas pulled her behind a tree and sternly instructed, "Stay here; do not move from this spot. If anything happens, call for me. Understand?"

"You can't face them alone," she argued. "They have weapons!"

"I'll be alright," he quickly responded. "Stay here and don't move!"

Reluctantly, she watched as Nicholas ran off and disappeared behind a cluster of gravestones. She was worried about him, and even though he had warned her not to move, she followed him deeper into the graveyard.

For a while, she lost sight of him. She hid behind a large tree, waiting to see what might happen next. Hearing voices from the east side of the graveyard, she discovered Nicholas facing the guns of Quinnley and Winkleman. She feared for his life and took a step towards him but was held back by two bony hands. She turned around, but there was no one there.

"Don't lapse into a life of corruption," Mary heard Nicholas say. "Give me the guns and your lives will be spared." But though it seemed that they hesitated, they did not lower their weapons. Their breathing was heavy as they stared into Nicholas's fiery eyes.

But they had both gone through too much to just give up now. Cocking his gun, Quinnley snarled, "I've killed one man already, and I'm not afraid to kill another." Next to him, Winkleman nodded. "I'm sorry, Nicholas," he said. Then they both shot at him.

Mary nearly screamed as tears erupted. She was afraid to look up, but she did, seeing Nicholas standing just as he was before. She was greatly astonished, as were the two murderers, since there clearly were two bullet marks in his chest. In the next instant, the holes disappeared before their very eyes!

They trembled in fear, seeing Nicholas advance on them. The two emptied their guns into him, but none of the shots affected the young undertaker. Their guns now useless, the two threw their weapons at him and turned to run.

With one sweeping motion of his hand, Nicholas directed a withering tree branch to fall and block the path of the escaping fugitives. The tree complied, and the branch dropped in the men's path, tripping them both.

They scrambled to their feet, only to find themselves again face-to-face with Nicholas Black.

They screamed, turning to run the other way, but were now blocked by a tall man dressed entirely in black. His face was shrouded, and without knowing why, Mr. Quinnley and Mr. Winkleman stared at it. Suddenly, a bare skull popped out and hissed at them, stopping their hearts cold. With his last breath, Quinnley tried to turn around, only to have his neck caught in Nicholas's grasp. The young man whispered threateningly to the officer, "I warned you."

Both men dropped dead, falling to the ground between Cairns and his son. Mary saw it all and could not believe her eyes. Her mouth fell open in shock and her entire body froze in fear. When Nicholas turned to look at her, she fainted right away.

Coming to her aid, Nicholas lifted her in his arms and looked anxiously towards his father. "Take her home," he directed his son. Young Nicholas obeyed and placed Mary in the hearse, transporting her to Wheaton Manor.

Chapter Thirty

*T*he next morning, Mary awoke to find herself safely in her room, tended to by her nurse. Dolly waited patiently as Mary emerged slowly from her state of shock, and watched as she fell back to her pillow, calming her racing heart as she struggled for words.

Dolly cooled her brow with a wet towel. "Calm yourself, Miss Wheaton," she said soothingly. "Everything's alright; calm down."

Taking her nurse's advice, Mary relaxed, allowed her pulse to return to normal and opened her eyes. She lay completely silent, going through the events of the previous night in her head, then felt the throb from the bump on the back of her skull.

Emitting a painful moan, she put a hand to the region and gently rubbed it. Drearily, she inquired, "What happened, Dolly?" Readjusting the girl's pillow, the nurse reached into the wash basin for the towel, and shook her head.

"You've received a nasty hit to the head, dear," she compassionately explained. "Mr. Black brought you home." Mary stirred.

"Mr. Black?" she repeated, then remembered arriving at Wheaton Manor late last night. She was barely conscious when Nicholas climbed the stairs to her room and set her gently down upon her bed. She put her left hand upon her right, recalling that he had kissed it before leaving. "Nicholas," she whispered. "I must go speak with him."

But Dolly pushed her back into bed as she attempted to get up. "No you don't, young miss," the nurse warned. "You must recover first before making any excursion into the outside world."

Mary was not up for a fight. The pounding in her head had returned. So, nodding to Dolly, she slipped under the covers. She was drained of all energy anyway and was soon fast asleep.

Dolly exited the room, closing the door behind her. Heading downstairs, she ran into Mr. Kent who inquired after Mary's health. "How is she?" he asked. Dolly lowered her head, worry written on her face. Mary was obviously going to survive, even though her nerves were shot.

"She's alright," Dolly replied. "But God knows what that child saw. I have never before seen her so frightened in my entire life. She could barely speak."

She tried to leave again but Mr. Kent stopped her. "Darlene," he said, eyes filled with sadness, "I need to speak to you." Nervously, Dolly looked at him, feeling her heart leap into her throat.

"So it was you," she said unexpectedly. Mr. Kent raised an eyebrow.

"What do you mean?" he asked.

"You went through my trunk while I was gone," she said. Cardew's eyes flew open.

"What?" he said. "I would never do you the dishonor."

"Then you have given the key to Mary," the maid concluded, with a feeling of relief. He didn't rat Mary out, but Dolly could see that it was so.

"She read my journal," Dolly continued. "And she told you what was in it." Cardew nodded, now that the truth was out. "Yes, Miss," he said.

Hurt, and unable to continue the conversation, he turned to depart to his room when Dolly spoke up. "I'm sorry, Cardew," she said. He stopped, standing there, close to tears. Then the tears streamed down his cheeks, and he shook his head, wanting to understand Dolly's motives.

"All I want to know is why?" he asked. "Why did you do it? We could have been married and settled with a family. Did I do something to displease you?"

Dolly felt tears form in her own eyes as she replied, "No, of course not, but…"

"Then, Why?!" he shouted. "Help me understand, Darlene. How could you destroy both our lives like that?"

Standing dumbly at Mary's door, Dolly felt the trickle of her tears. "I did get married," she replied. "But my husband died early on. Before I came to Wheaton Manor, I had a son. He was a strong and healthy boy until…"

She completely broke down then and cried. Mr. Kent came over to console her. "I was angry and scared," she continued. "I didn't want to…relive that."

Holding her in his arms just like when they were young, he comforted her. Wiping away her tears, he soothingly whispered to her, "You'll never face anything alone again. I promise."

She had been holding him tightly, but now she stepped away and looked up at him in confusion. Eyes filled with tears, she asked him, "What do you mean?" Gently, he placed both his hands on her face, and laid his forehead against hers.

"Marry me," he whispered softly.

Chapter Thirty-One

*T*he town was in an uproar when they learned that Mr. Quinnley and Mr. Winkleman were the grave robbers all along. They had been thought of as upright individuals and exemplary gentlemen, incapable of doing wrong.

Mrs. Parker, too, was in shock. She continued to argue with Mr. Adams that it couldn't be so, because Thomas Winkleman had been so close to her husband. "They were always together," she said, with a sad look in her eyes. "Louis treated him like a son, and Thomas regarded him as a father. He spoke at the funeral, you know. His heart was torn to shreds upon learning of Louis's murder."

But Mr. Adams, grief-stricken himself, assured the widow that the reports were just as he had told her. "I understand your surprise, Mrs. Parker," he declared, "but they attacked Miss Mary Wheaton and the undertaker's son. Good thing those kids were able to get away, or we would have had a few more murders on our hands."

Now understanding the reality of what had happened, the widow cried, feeling the pain deep in her heart. "Is there no virtue left on this earth?" she sobbed.

Wanting to hear nothing more of the occurrences of the previous night, the old woman imprisoned herself in her home, with only her servants for company.

Mr. Adams left devastated, returning to his empty home in gloom, and sat staring at Quinnley's things which were just a few feet away. He felt that Norbert was like the son he had always wanted: loyal, self-sacrificing, and obedient. If only Quinnley had kept to the scruples that he preached.

But Webster didn't want to take the route Mrs. Parker decided to assume and keep to his house. Rather, he sat in the church for the next couple of days and prayed, wondering where his next step in life would lead him.

As he sat in the front pew of the church, his face covered, Mary walked in and found him in deep prayer. He was crying, she could tell. She did not interrupt him as she sat silently next to him, eyes closed, immersed in her own disappointment.

It was a sunny day outside and the birds weaved in and out of the colorful leaves on the old oaks. The town was busy as usual: the children danced and played, while their parents labored in the kitchens and yards. The graveyard was the only silent spot around. Death rested soundly, just as the sounds of silence swept into the hearts of Mary and Mr. Adams.

The church was dark, save for the two candles. They raised their eyes up to the cross and stared, wondering in their hearts what to do next.

But with a deep breath, the officer broke the silence. "Not the most pleasant of days, Miss Wheaton," he said as he tried to compose himself. Mary turned to him and nodded sadly.

"No it isn't, Mr. Adams," she replied, then continued sitting quietly.

He rested his hand on hers, continuing to gaze at the cross. Suddenly, he felt the girl's fingers wrap around his. His tears subsiding, he turned to her and said, "I suspect you're leaving, Miss Wheaton." The girl turned towards him but avoided his eyes.

"Is it any surprise?" she asked. The officer shook his head.

"Of course not," he gloomily responded. "The undertakers are leaving as well."

Mary's eyes met his. "The Blacks are leaving?" she repeated, and the officer nodded.

"Yes," he confirmed. "In fact, I think they've left already."

Hastily genuflecting, Mary hurried out of the church. She didn't know why, but she wanted to talk with Nicholas -- perhaps to thank him before he left. She knew that he spent much of his time outdoors, but unable to find him working at any of the gravesites, she headed for the workshop where the coffins were fashioned, and rushed in.

The foyer was empty, but coats still hung on the stand, which gave her hope that the Blacks might not have left just yet. Entering the workshop area, Mary found Nicholas's working space cleared of any sawdust. The tools were neatly placed in their proper locations and the wood planks stacked according to size underneath the window.

She frowned, losing her hope at that instant, and stood teary eyed. On one hand, she was somewhat relieved that she didn't have to speak to him, but she felt remorseful that he was leaving. Turning to leave the workshop, she jumped when the elder Mr. Black suddenly appeared.

As he approached her, he withdrew his hands from his pockets and lightly slid his glove across one of the cutting tables. His face was covered, as it normally was. Stopping in front of her, he asked, "What are you doing here?"

Mary looked at him, thinking how peculiar his accent was, and stood mute for a moment before she found herself saying, "I'm looking for Nicholas."

Cairns took off his hat and overcoat and put them on the stand by the door. Mary now saw that he looked like a normal human with skin and organs. This puzzled her, because in the moonlight, he was nothing but bone.

Approaching him, she inquired again about the whereabouts of his son.

He didn't reply. Instead, he touched the newly potted violet plant. Instantly, it withered and died, shriveling into dust. The soil that it was potted in dried up as well.

Startled by this demonstration, Mary still tried to appear outwardly calm. Cairns turned his attention to her, while her heart pounded mercilessly against her chest. It seemed as if he was enjoying the silent torture he was inflicting upon her.

He eventually broke his silence, anxious to have her leave the premises as soon as possible. "Why do you need to speak with my son?"

"A personal matter," Mary replied, not knowing what else she could say. Quickly, Cairns shook his head.

"No," he replied and walked to the foyer. Mary followed him, confused.

"Why ever not?" she demanded to know. Mr. Black turned toward her, and Mary could see his fiery eyes.

"Miss Wheaton," he said, "do you know what we are?" Mary shrugged her shoulders. "Let me show you." He slowly withdrew one of his gloves. Mary waited, wondering what he would do to her. He took her hand in his, and immediately Mary felt a sharp pain surge through her hand. She looked down, wondering what might be wrong, and was horrified to find that her skin and tissues were evaporating; she could now actually see her bones.

With a frightened scream, she pulled her hand away from his, and was then pleasantly surprised to see it slowly return to normal. This scared her, as she protected her hand from further contact with his. She watched as he casually placed his glove back on.

"What are you?" she asked, barely breathing.

He smiled, though his eyes were sinister. He moved closer to her, and she backed away. "I'm the Grim Reaper, Miss Wheaton," he said. "Death, in the flesh."

Mary was dumbfounded, shaking her head in disbelief. Could it be that all the stories Mr. Rodchester had told her about this family were true? If so, then she was in for the ride of her life.

"You're immortal, then?" she asked. Cairns nodded. "The reason for the 'Black Death'?" she pushed on.

"Well it wasn't called the 'Black Death' for nothing," the undertaker replied. "Our name is right in the title. But the Asians had it coming."

"It affected many Europeans as well."

"I know. They had it coming too."

"So you hate mortals."

"What? Because of the Bubonic Plague? No."

"Then why won't you let me talk to Nicholas?"

Cairns stopped and glared at her. Mary took a step back, thinking that he was going to explode into a ball of fire. But Mr. Black restrained his fury, and stood silently for a moment before he said, "There are two reasons. Reason one…"

Swinging his hand in a sweeping motion from left to right, he caused the room to erupt in a whirlwind of fire. The workshop disappeared completely. In its place, there appeared blue skies and lush green fields full of exotic plant life. Beautiful stonework rose before Mary's astonished eyes, and the sun briefly exploded with brilliant rays of light, before subsiding to its normal state.

When everything had finally settled down, Cairns placed his hands behind his back and said, "Welcome to Athens, Greece, 1242 B.C."

The architecture looked like it was alive, which was so much more pleasing to the eye than ancient ruins. Women were decorated with golden bands and jewelry not seen for centuries. The men looked strong, and strolled around discussing their ideas with philosophers and thinkers.

Mr. Black drew her attention to a beautiful Grecian woman who emerged from the green fields of the thriving city. She had long, flowing, blond hair and her eyes were like pools of liquid chocolate. Her smile beamed brighter than the jewels that adorned her body. She skipped across the fields and leapt into the arms of a man whom Mary deduced was Cairns.

He looked very young, appearing to be about the age of his son, and was exceptionally handsome. His hair was dark red and his face free of any scars. His body was very well-built and his eyes a penetrating blue.

He spun the beautiful woman around before gently setting her down on the ground. They kissed, then proceeded to stroll happily into the city, stopping occasionally to listen to some of the discussions taking place.

"Now pay attention," Cairns advised Mary as he swung his hand around again. Suddenly day turned to night, and Mary saw the Grecian woman walking alone along a forest's edge. She was gazing peacefully at the moon when she was confronted by two criminals who emerged from the woods. She screamed as she tried to get away from them. But they grabbed her by the hair and ripped all the precious jewels and gold off her. She cried out for help, and to her great relief, someone came running to her aid. Looking closely, Mary saw the young Cairns approaching the criminals in just the same way as he had earlier confronted Quinnley and Winkleman. He did not appear to be human, as his bones shone in the moonlight.

He ordered the men to stop. They froze in terror, staring into Cairns' empty eye sockets. Paralyzed with fear, they dropped everything as every last breath was drained from them. Their eyes rolled back in their heads, and they fell to the ground dead.

The Grecian woman watched the unfolding drama in astonishment. She got up, peering to the skeleton in both gratitude and fear, and nearly ran away before the frame swung around and faced her. "Ana," he said to her in a familiar tone. "It's me, Cairns."

Ana shook her head in astonishment, feeling the urge to run, but Mr. Black blocked her path. He stood firmly and said, "Ana, it really is me. Come; I'll prove it to you."

Hesitantly, she followed Cairns into the shadow of a laurel tree and watched as he transformed into a human figure right before her very eyes.

Still finding it hard to believe what she had just witnessed, she gently touched his face, and said, "Cairns? What are you?"

Grasping her hand, he gazed into her eyes and said, "I'm the Grim Reaper." She drew her hand away and stood fear-stricken before him.

"You're Death?" she exhaled. "Why are you human only in sunlight and in the shadows?"

"I'm thousands of years old," he told her. "I show my true form at night." Approaching her, he said, "Ana, please don't hate me. I'm the same Cairns you knew when we first met. I can make you immortal, and we can be together until the end of time."

Her curiosity was aroused, and soon her breathing returned to normal. Cairns reached for her hand, and as she gazed into his deep, blue eyes, he said, "You must promise to love me forever if you want to live forever."

A smile crossed her face as she nodded in agreement. Suddenly, Greece faded into the Reaper's memory. Traveling through time, Mr. Black said, "We were married before the Dorians attacked. We fled to Italy for a while, and that's when Nicholas was born."

Gradually, a vision of a healthy baby boy came briefly into view, before fading again. Mr. Black continued, "But Ana and I were only married one hundred years before she broke her end of the bargain."

Looking past Cairns' hand, Mary saw the vast Roman Empire emerge from a cloud of dust. Loud cheers rose all around her, and looking towards an area specifically set aside for fighting, she found a massive crowd gathered to cheer on the gladiators in the ring. One man had golden armor, the other silver. The man with the golden armor clearly had the advantage over his opponent. He was strongly built, and displayed perfect footwork and masterful swordsmanship. The other, a skinny individual with barely any muscle on him, was quick with his strikes, but he lacked consistency.

It all ended quickly and the man in golden armor waited for the signal to slay his competitor. It was soon given, and without any hesitation, he ended his opponent's life.

The audience roared with delight, and bowing to his adoring fans, the gladiator disappeared into a nearby building and went to his private room to remove his armor. When he entered, Ana approached him from behind, and removed his helmet. Startled, he turned around, and drew his sword, but found that it was a young Grecian woman. "Lower your weapon," Ana said to him as she tossed aside his helmet. He did so and soon their lips made contact.

"Ana didn't know that I was among the spectators that day," Cairns said to Mary. "I wanted to congratulate the victor, since I hadn't seen fighting like that in ages. Entering the gladiator's room, I found Ana in the arms of Arminius of Atlantis. They looked at me, discomfited."

"Cairns!" the woman exclaimed. "What are you doing here?"

"What am I doing here?!" Mr. Black repeated, angrily. "I'm Death! Arminius slew Galgamay. Weren't you watching? Or were you too busy locking lips with this Neanderthal to care?"

"Cairns…," the woman tried to explain, but was silenced when the Reaper bellowed, "Enough!" The entire structure shook from his furious cry and Arminius fell to the ground, dead.

Approaching his wife, he shouted, "Your vows were broken in the sight of God. End this life, this adulterous façade!"

Instantaneously, Ana fell to the ground dead, and disintegrated. The entire building soon collapsed and the vision vanished. Mary, observing as the fires spun once again, saw one last image of Cairns and his son at Ana's gravesite before her present reality returned.

Feeling the ground form under her feet and the walls climb up around her, Mary found herself back in the workshop at the St. Xavier's Cemetery. Cairns stood quietly beside her.

"I drowned Atlantis not long after," he said. Mary looked at him sympathetically. But she was still angry that he would not let her speak to his son.

"So you won't let me speak with Nicholas because of what happened to you ages ago?" she concluded. Cairns raised his head.

"Don't take any offense, Miss Wheaton," the Reaper said to her. "Nicholas and I cannot develop any relationships with mortals. I want to prevent him from experiencing the pain that I endure to this very day. A little part of you dies when a mortal passes."

"But that's Nicholas's choice, not yours," Mary argued. "He's old enough to make his own decisions."

"But *you're* not immortal, Miss Wheaton," Cairns pointed out.

Mary stared at him, but did not argue further. Collecting herself, she said, "Alright. What is the second reason?"

Glaring at her, Cairns motioned Mary to the funeral parlor and she followed him. The Reaper reached down behind the podium for a music book. He approached her and gestured for her to look. Opening the book, she found that every single page was blank.

She was confused, her brow furrowed. Turning towards him, she looked inquiringly, wondering what it was that he wanted her to see. "It's blank," she said, still flipping through the pages. "There's nothing in here."

"Look a bit closer," Cairns directed, and returning to the empty pages, Mary saw musical notes begin to form before her very eyes; then the bars assembled. Soon, an entire song jumbled its way onto the page. Rays of light emanated from the book, and the title emerged, *'A Drunkard's Reel'*.

Absolutely astonished, Mary placed a hand on the page and touched the notes. They felt inky, as if they had just been written. Peering up at the undertaker, she asked, "What is this?" Closing the book, Mr. Black pointed to the cover.

"*'The Book of Death'*," he said to her. "Every time an individual is supposed to die, a song appears in the book, and I play it. Each song is special to that person; no two songs are alike."

"I fail to see your reasoning for showing this to me," Mary commented. Mr. Black looked irritated.

"You are an impatient little girl, aren't you?" he declared.

Swiping his hand over the book, he caused the pages to flip furiously until they were halfway through the book. Mary waited for the notes to assemble, then, looking at the top of the page, she read, '*A Waltz of Innocence: Rosemary Wheaton*'.

She stared at the words, reading them over and over to herself. Looking up, she thought she understood their significance. "You see," Cairns explained, "this song appeared in the book three days ago. I played it, yet somehow you're still alive. Now why do you suppose that is?" The girl shrugged her shoulders.

"Perhaps it wasn't my time," she said with an awkward smile. Cairns glared at her with skepticism.

"Look in the right hand corner of the book," he instructed.

Mary peered closely, and saw a date appear: *29 September 1845*. "That was yesterday," she breathed. The Reaper closed the book and put it back in its rightful place. He gazed at her most seriously and tapped his fingers on the podium. Then, his hands behind his back, he began to pace the room.

"As the Grim Reaper," he started, "it is my job to ensure that death occurs. With all the deaths that do take place, you're probably wondering how I keep an eye on all those souls. I could manage it alone, but it is a tremendous help when Nicholas lends a hand. He's somewhat of a Reaper, even though his humanity dominates his nature. He helps to guarantee that all individuals meet their fate. But for some strange reason, you seemed to have escaped his watchful eye."

Mary looked away, gasping. He turned to face her, eyes sparkling and lips widening to a smile. Walking back to the podium, he rested one hand on top as he stared at her. "I can't let you live forever, now, can I?" he stated in fearsome satisfaction. "But you missed your time. What should I do, Miss Wheaton? Hmm?"

Looking away, Mary swallowed the rest of her fear, searching for courage. Butterflies were dancing in her stomach, and her mind pounded with anticipation.

But she looked directly into the Grim Reaper's eyes, and with all the courage she could muster, said, "I want to speak to Nicholas and there's nothing you can do to stop me. I don't care if you kill me before I get the chance. I will merely haunt him and get my message across to him one way or another."

Pushing right through him, Cairns disappeared into a smoky, black cloud. Mary entered the workshop to continue her search for Nicholas. The room was still empty, so she proceeded towards the back room.

Quite unexpectedly, Nicholas emerged from the back, a sanding block in his hands. He halted when he saw her, and his jaw dropped. "Rosemary?" he breathed in astonishment. She stopped, supporting herself on the door frame. She saw the young man in a white shirt, black pants, and with an apron about his waist.

He laid the sanding block on a nearby ledge as he slowly approached her. Mary shook with every breath that she took, staring into his eyes as he came closer and closer to her, completely lost for words.

She was filled with mixed emotions. Nicholas's eyes were empathetic as he bowed hesitantly. In an even tone, she said, "Oh, so now you're on speaking terms with me?" The young man wiped his hands together nervously and untied his apron, tossing it on a table nearby.

"Miss Wheaton," the boy replied tensely, "believe me. The last thing I wanted to do was to hurt you."

"Then why did you," Mary retorted. "Was it because of your father's rule?" Nicholas's shoulders drooped.

"You spoke with my father?" he asked, rather apprehensively. Mary nodded.

"Your father showed me his interesting past with your mother," she explained. "And might I say, he made absolutely no sense. Now he wants to sever all ties with the world. But what I don't understand is why did *you* have to be so uncivil towards me?"

For a long while, Nicholas was silent. He stared into her determined eyes, while internally, he searched for a suitable answer. He did not wish to be unkind, yet he felt that he had to respond to her in such a way that she would never speak to him again. That was the way to sever ties with the world, whether he agreed with them or not.

She waited for his reply. He trembled, fighting in his head with his father, while he gazed into her beautiful, green eyes.

"My father wanted all ties with the world severed right away," he finally blurted out. "I had to be uncivil so you wouldn't talk to me again."

"You could have civilly told me that you didn't want to talk to me," Mary countered. "I would have left you alone."

"I couldn't do that."

"Why?"

"I just couldn't!"

"But why, Nicholas!"

With frustration reaching its peak, Nicholas cried out, "Because I love you!" Not at all expecting such a response, Mary could only stare at him in astonishment. Her eyes followed him as he nervously paced the room, running his fingers through his hair. He could not believe what he had just told her.

Confused, Mary shook her head. "I don't understand," she confessed. "What does that have to do with…"

"It has everything to do with my actions," Nicholas interrupted. "Don't you see, Rosemary? I had to break your heart in order to break my own. You *are* my world."

Mary was dumbfounded, as Nicholas now approached her. She had never heard another person utter such sweetness in her entire life. She felt tears rush to her eyes, and her heart beat violently in her chest. Nicholas was becoming teary eyed as well.

"I love you," he said again, in all sincerity. Mary gazed into his eyes and swallowed her apprehension.

"I love you too, Nicholas," she replied, choking on her own tears. Overjoyed, Nicholas grabbed her in his arms and kissed her, as tears streamed down their faces.

"I'm sorry," he said between kisses. "I'm so sorry, Rosemary."

They were still locked in a loving embrace when suddenly Mary jumped. "Will you stop doing that?" she shouted at the elder Mr. Black.

Pushing Mary behind him, Nicholas turned to face his father, and said to Cairns, "I don't care what you say; I love her."

But Mr. Black didn't appear upset or disappointed at this declaration. Rather, he exhaled and smiled, saying to his son, "Then get on with it." Mary and Nicholas exchanged confused glances.

"What do you mean?" the boy asked, puzzled, while tightly gripping Mary's arm. Cairns showed no emotion.

"Ask her," he said to his son.

Nicholas was greatly troubled and glared at his father to determine whether there was trickery in his eyes or not. Seeing none, he was thrown into even greater confusion. Releasing Mary from his grasp, he asked his father, "What's the catch?"

"No catch, son," the Reaper responded. "You didn't really think I could prevent you from falling in love, did you? I just wanted you to be extra sure about it. And seeing the young woman you have chosen, I admit, I like her very much as well."

Nicholas closed his eyes and threw his head back. "You set me up!" he cried. "I can't believe this." Then he added, "Actually, I *can* believe this. Are you insane?!"

"A bit," Cairns said, gesturing, "but that's what you get when your father's the Grim Reaper."

When Nicholas's emotions had settled down, he turned to Mary, smiled, and took her hands into his own. She looked up at him contentedly, a little disturbed that she had fallen for the Grim Reaper's son, but overjoyed that she had finally found a man who cared for her as much as Nicholas did. She really and truly loved him. And her surprises seemed to have no end when Nicholas asked her, "Rosemary Wheaton, will you accept my hand in holy matrimony?"

Her hand flew to her mouth in shock. She stared long and hard into his eyes, before responding, "But you're immortal. How will you…"

"My father is willing to make you immortal too, just like he made my mother," Nicholas gently explained. "So what do you say?"

Mary didn't honestly know what to say. Everything was hitting her all at once, but she knew what she wanted now. Everything had become clear to her. Gently caressing his cheek, she kissed him and replied, "Yes."

Absolutely thrilled, Nicholas was about to hug her again when she stopped him. "*But*, first you have to talk to Mr. Adams and get his consent. My father had entrusted that duty to him before he died."

"Where is he?" the boy inquired excitedly.

"In the church," Mary said. "He's sitting in the front pew."

Nicholas went off to take care of this matter, leaving Mary in the room with Cairns. She smiled, now in complete rapture that she was going to be a married woman, and thanked the Reaper for all his help. "You have proven my notions about you to be wrong, Mr. Reaper," she said to him. "I thank you for everything."

She was making ready to leave when Cairns held out a hand to her. "Not so fast, Miss Wheaton," he said to her. "I still need to grant you your immortality. Give me your hands."

A bit reluctantly, Mary placed her hands in the Reaper's palms and waited, squinting with the fear that this would sting. "Is it going to hurt?" she asked him. He looked at her.

"What?"

"The process," she responded. "Is it going to hurt?"

"I did it already," he said. She tilted her head.

"Really?"

"No," he chuckled, as Mary's body was jolted with what seemed like thousands of volts of electricity. She was caught off guard by the power generated within her system by his action. Cairns laughed, showing no sympathy, while she tried to catch her breath, twitching about the room. "You're going to have a little tick for a while," he called out to her. "But don't worry, it eventually goes away. Maybe."

Leaving her with these words, the Reaper disappeared in a black cloud of mist and returned to his work. Mary waited where she was, hoping that Mr. Adams would send his blessing upon her, because she knew that another Nicholas would never come her way.

Chapter Thirty-Two

*F*or the first time in ages, Nicholas felt happy. Joy surged through his system, a feeling he had never experienced before. He smiled, thinking how astounding it was that after thousands of years, he was able to find a woman like Mary. He had never imagined himself falling in love, let alone getting married. He had stoically focused on his duties; that is, until he had met Miss Wheaton.

Returning to his regular character, he now entered the church, and located Mr. Adams, just as Mary had told him. Hesitantly, he walked to the front pew, and genuflected before sitting down. He raised his eyes to the cross. Mr. Adams was lost in his own world, and did not realize who was sitting next to him. He buried his face in his hands, deep in prayer.

Yet Nicholas was patient; that was his forte. He quietly rested his hands in his lap, and said a few prayers silently. Suddenly, the officer jerked out of his trance. Mr. Adams must have thought that Mary had returned, because he put his hand on the undertaker's. Nicholas looked down in surprise, and Mr. Adams soon realized his error.

"Oh sorry, son!" he apologized. "I thought you were Miss Wheaton." He tapped his hands on his lap uncomfortably. Nicholas did not stir. The officer, on the other hand, was restless. He tried to return to his prayers, but was distracted by the undertaker's presence next to him. He wasn't sure why Nicholas was sitting next to him, or why he was even in the chapel in the first place. The young man broke the silence, sensing Mr. Adams' anxiety.

"I'm sorry about what happened," he said quietly. The officer raised his head and stared at him sadly.

"Oh," he replied, after a long pause, "it wasn't your fault. Quinnley chose his path and he suffered for it. The chap let greed overcome him to the point where his disregard for life clouded his better judgment. The important thing is that you and Miss Wheaton are safe."

He lowered his head again, not caring for his present company. Nicholas sensed that, but persisted anyway, "What about you? What are your feelings?"

Mr. Adams stirred. "I don't know, but I can't change fate."

Quietly, they sat in the pew, feeling the silence, and stared ahead of them awkwardly. The officer did his best to ignore the undertaker.

Much as he wanted to leave, Nicholas stayed where he was. Suddenly, an idea crossed his mind. Turning to the officer he asked tentatively, "May I be frank with you, sir?" Mr. Adams looked up, interested in what he might have to say, and nodded. Nicholas continued, "You are horrible at hiding your emotions." The old man stared at him.

"Is that so?" he asked. "Why would you say that?" Nicholas shrugged.

"You're like a book, sir," the boy calmly replied. "I can see how the chapters are a mass of confusion, how they're searching for order. I can see your heart is aching at the mere thought of Miss Rosemary leaving. You want nothing more than her happiness, but you ask yourself if it's selfish to feel happiness too. You're confounded, worried, and incensed that everything is jumbled up and landing in your lap. You're scared, asking God to give you the strength to endure your cross as life drags on. And, as I sit with you right now, I can feel your resentment for me seep through every vein in your body as you wonder how I know so much about you."

Mr. Adams was astonished. All those feelings that had been boxed away within his heart, everything that he thought he could easily hide under a mask of seriousness, had been effortlessly revealed by someone he hardly ever spoke with. People that he had known for years could never do what Nicholas had just done. Looking over towards Nicholas in wonder, the officer asked, "How did you do that?"

"It's part of the job," the undertaker said somberly. "You learn to read people over time."

"Just like that?" the officer queried. Nicholas concurred.

"Just like that."

The old man's disposition towards Nicholas was transformed from discomfort to open admiration. He thought that he might try to discover the young undertaker's secret.

"Let me try," he said, staring at Nicholas, trying to read his emotions. He should have known better, because the undertaker always maintained the same serious face.

He next looked intently into Nicholas's brown eyes, and he saw both mischief and compassion in them. The emotions shifted, based on how Nicholas was feeling, and Mr. Adams was quick to point that out.

"You're in love," he said finally, tilting his head to get a better look.

"Very good," the young man replied and Webster went on, scratching at his head and beard as he pondered further.

"And you either want to tell me something, or you're ready to slug me."

"The former," Nicholas offered. The officer sat up.

"You're not in love with me, are you?" Nicholas glared at him.

"No," he said. "Try again."

The old officer struggled, unable to read anything more definitive than this, yet curious to know who the lady might be. He scrolled through several possibilities in his mind's eye, mentally checking the compatibility of each pair. But he could see Nicholas matched with no one other than Mary, since she was the only woman he had ever been with.

Finally, with an aching sensation in his stomach, he concluded, "You're in love with Mary." Nicholas's eyes widened. "You came here to get my consent," the officer continued, and Nicholas nodded.

Mr. Adams stood up and began pacing in the aisle, running his hand through his hair, and finding it hard to accept the circumstance he now found himself in. He had been prepared to expect that some day a gentleman would ask for Mary's hand, but he did not expect that that individual would turn out to be the undertaker's son.

He was fearful, wishing not to speak, and the boy was quick to sense his uneasiness. "Don't be upset, sir," the young man said. "I assure you that I love Rosemary more than you could ever imagine." The officer looked surprised.

"Why do you love her?" he countered. Nicholas pondered the question a few moments before venturing a response. There were so many reasons, and too little time to explain them all.

"To be plain," he said with a shy smile, "I've been lost in the dark and desolate world of bleak vocations, unaware that I was longing for a light to guide me out of that gloom. When Rosemary came along, the heavy clouds of despondency vanished away the instant I saw her radiant smile. From that moment forth, hers was the only face I'd see in a crowded room, the only voice I'd hear among hundreds, and the only woman I could ever love. Words, however, are boundaries for the feelings that I hold in my heart, Mr. Adams. If you could really understand how I felt, you'd die of happiness."

Mr. Adams was left speechless. Though he might not feel what the young undertaker was feeling, he was sure by the way Nicholas spoke about Rosemary that he was madly in love with her. He felt tears fill his eyes as he watched the young lover wait for a response. He struggled to contain all the emotions that were suddenly rushing through every fiber of his being.

And so, turning to Nicholas, he extended his hand, knowing that the young man would take good care of Mary. Words could not begin to describe the sensation that flowed through the young man as he shook Mr. Adams' hand and heard him say, "I can think of no better match for Miss Rosemary, Mr. Black. You have my consent."

Nicholas shook his head in disbelief while a big smile crossed his face and tears rolled down his cheeks. "Thank you," he said, full of gratitude. "Thank you so much."

He hugged Mr. Adams, shook his hand again, genuflected before the tabernacle, then rushed out of the church. The officer stood alone, sighing from both relief and cheer. He realized suddenly that he hadn't lost a daughter after all. In fact, he now had two children who would remain steadfast to the end. Outwardly he might try to deny it, but he really was quite fond of Nicholas Black - - also known as the Grim Reaper's son.

Perhaps trickery played a role in uniting Nicholas Black and Rosemary Wheaton. But the two were too much in love to hold a grudge against their father, Cairns. They were married the following week, with the entire village of Denny's Grove in attendance. Several members of the congregation were shocked to see Mary marrying an undertaker, considering it quite untoward for her to do so. She, however, didn't care two straws about their opinions as the pair exchanged vows before God, she hardly able to contain her pleasure when the priest announced her new title: Mrs. Nicholas Black.

As for the others: Mr. Ferzley proposed to Morgan upon his return from the Punjab Empire where the British scored a rather easy victory. They set their wedding date for the sixteenth of June, 1846, by which time Nicholas and Rosemary were already expecting their first child.

After twenty-seven years of playing cat and mouse, Dolly agreed to wed Mr. Kent on the seventh of February,

1846. Cardew claimed he was the happiest man alive. Nicholas begged to differ, knowing full well that no person alive could ever understand the limitless love of an immortal.

And lastly came the Grim Reaper, who was not as grim as everyone had thought him to be. Yes, he was the dealer of death, but he was reasonable, knowing that there was a higher authority than his own. He developed a close relationship with his new daughter-in-law from the day she said 'I do', and delightfully teased her as she slowly grew accustomed to her immortality. He was happy to enjoy family life again, though he tried to hide his contentment behind a mask of solemnity. He no longer rushed Judgment Day, savored every passing moment, knowing that it wouldn't be forever until time ended.

About the Author

Elizabeth Fortini was born in Kenosha, Wisconsin, and grew up in Ballwin, Missouri where she began to write at the young age of seven. It wasn't until she moved back to Wisconsin that she discovered her love for writing. "At fourteen, I was experimenting with a WWII novel. I gave writing a rest for a while until I rewrote the novel at age sixteen, finishing it a year later. I felt like I accomplished something so wonderful that I knew I wanted to be a writer." Now eighteen, Elizabeth is out of school. She hopes that by writing novels, she can bring joy to others as their happiness brings joy to her. "These writings are my gift to God. I hope that by putting my heart into every work that I write that they will be sufficient offerings to Him."

www.ingramcontent.com/pod-product-compliance
Lightning Source LLC
Chambersburg PA
CBHW030031180626
46810CB00001B/309